ERIMEM

ABSOLUTION

Rachel Blake

from a story by Iain McLaughlin and Claire Bartlett

Erimem: Absolution © Rachel Blake
Editor: Julianne Todd
Range Editor: Iain McLaughlin
First published in 2020
Erimem and associated concepts Copyright © 2020 Iain McLaughlin
All rights reserved.
Cover photograph by Dorina Petco
No part of this publication may be reproduced, stored in a retrieval system or
transmitted in any form or by any means, electronic, mechanical, photocopying,
recording or any other manner without prior written permission of the copyright
holder.
First published in 2020 by Thebes Publishing
follow us online:
www.thebespublishing.com
https://www.facebook.com/ThebesPublishing
https://twitter.com/ThebesNews
ISBN: 978-1-910868-36-2

THEBES PUBLISHING

ERIMEM

ABSOLUTION

PROLOGUE

Peace came to the Venulatu system in an unlikely way.

For almost five hundred years the twin worlds Prenual and Sarvin had been engaged in a bitter conflict. The worlds were only nine million kilometres apart and both orbited the binary suns at the heart of their system.

It had always seemed something of a coincidence that humanoids had evolved on both planets at the same time, which led scholars on both worlds to believe that there had to be some kind of link between the worlds. Unfortunately, that theory cut little ice with the leaders on either planet. Ever since they had become aware of each other's existence there had been a mutual animosity. No-one could quite remember what had caused it but everyone knew that it was the other side who had started it.

The two planets developed rudimentary space travel at around the same time. Prenual, which was the inner of the two worlds, sent a ship to observe their neighbour. It was not met with friendship. And so, for hundreds of years the planets remained at loggerheads. The patterns and rhythms of the two planets' orbits meant that the worlds were often too far apart, sometimes even on the opposing sides of the suns, and the situation dimmed to a gnawing acrimony but when the worlds drew closer, their burgeoning space fleets came into contact – and into conflict.

Both planets had set about exploring and colonising the rest of their solar system. This was also the cause of a great deal of rancour with the planets lodging claims and counter-claims on planets, moons and asteroids.

The system had six gas giants out beyond the orbit of Sarvin. The second largest was named Brun by the people of Sarvin and for some reason, Prenual had simply named it Bob. It was a name which mean "life-giver" in an ancient dialect. To others, later in history, it would simply mean cheap laughs.

Klemmer had once been a planet back in the early years of the solar system's existence but as the planets had moved and aligned themselves, fitting into the natural gravitational order of the system, Klemmer had been dragged from its own orbit, gently captured by Brun – or Bob – as it shifted position. In that moment it had become the largest moon in the system. It was also the most interesting, possessing an oxygen-nitrogen atmosphere and the ideal surface conditions for life. Both Prenual and Sarvin decided that Klemmer was ideal for colonisation and despatched ships to the moon. Both worlds forged outposts and threatened to land colonists. Spaceships fought skirmishes in orbit and troops had scuffled on the planet's unexpectedly lush surface. Tensions increased as ships were lost and troops were killed. The Emperor of Prenual sent his finest general to oversee the battle. In response, the King of Sarvin sent his most famous warrior to secure a final victory.

The two armies gathered to face battle on the Plain of Borth, one of the most naturally beautiful places anyone in the universe would ever see. A thick carpet of lush grass surrounded on three sides by trees and with Brun – or Bob – and its system of rings half visible above, filling a good third of the sky.

Before the battle would commence, the two leaders met to offer the other side the chance to surrender like the cowards they were.

The soldiers waited outside while the two leaders met in private in a tent set up for their discussions. While soldiers waited... and waited... and waited outside for the war to begin, the two leaders surrendered to each other and to fate.

The Emperor of Prenual's finest general was his daughter, Miri. She was tall with flowing red hair and intelligent green eyes. Sarvin's great warrior was the king's oldest daughter Sanna, whose heart was reputed to be as black as her hair.

The two leaders met in private in the tent, as was the custom... and they fell in love. The attraction was immediate, the chemistry instant and the outcome unavoidable. Both leaders stood down their armies and sent them home. They arranged to meet with their fathers on a neutral asteroid and told the old men that their two greatest warriors wished to be married.

War was an expensive business and the two great leaders agreed to the marriage. After months of negotiations it was agreed that the ceremony would take place on a specially built space station at the exact midpoint between the two worlds at the time of the marriage so that neither world would see the event first.

The marriage was televised on every channel across both worlds. Nobody had ever seen the two generals ever look so happy. Their fathers stood side by side and shared a few jokes and laughs. When the happy couple kissed after finalising their vows, both planets sang to the sounds of cheers and bells being tolled. It was the happiest day in the system's history.

The two enemies had ended hostilities.

Celebrations were declared for three days on the two planets and all of their moons, outposts and space stations. Everyone drank and ate and danced as if there was no tomorrow.

For most of them there really was no tomorrow.

The first of the blood-red ships dropped into normal space late in the night of the first day of celebrations. Without warning it blasted a Prenual space station to oblivion. Moments later a Sarvin colony dropped out of contact.

A fleet of red ship appeared without warning at every outpost of either world and blasted them from existence. There were no communications, no responses to the pleas for mercy or assistance. There was simply a relentless, merciless attack which only stopped when the target was obliterated.

The red ships spread like a plague, wiping out the burgeoning expires of both worlds until it was only those two worlds that remained. The two leaders joined their fleets into one giant force to take a stance against these invaders.

It was a slaughter.

The joint fleet was destroyed within an hour. Every ship was devastated and left floating dead in space.

The red fleet surrounded the two worlds and in unison opened fire. The surface of both planets were ravaged and scorched. The bombardments lasted for two days. At the end, when the red fleet broke orbit, there was no-one alive on either planet.

On its way out of the system the red fleet stopped at the space station where the marriage had taken place. The two brides and some of their guests were the only people aboard. There hadn't been time or room on the ships to ferry them back to their fleets.

The red fleet surrounded the station and held position as if staring at it, deciding what to do.

The onslaught was brutal. A dozen ships opened fire. The newly married couple had time to hold hands just a little tighter before the station erupted in a fireball.

The red fleet turned and eased away through space before making a jump into faster than light travel. Behind them the ships left carnage and billions of corpses in a dead system.

Peace had finally come to the Venulatu system.

And it was terrible.

CHAPTER ONE

The great starliner, the *RSL Andromedan Princess*, was one of the last ships built by the legendary shipyards of New Govan, before that vast space station in orbit around Mars was repurposed as a habitat and commercial location... a town floating in space.

The *Andromedan Princess* passed serenely through space on a seven planet and four space station tour spread over two weeks. It was an enormous ship with over three thousand passengers and the same number of crew aboard. The ship was the zenith of upper class luxury, its stylings based on those of the great ocean liners of early Twentieth Century Earth, in particular the White Star line.

The *Andromedan Princess* was due to arrive at Harker's Pleasure Station later in the morning. Ships in space tended to cling to GMT as a base for time-keeping and the *Andromedan Princess* stuck with that tradition.

Portia Lescal looked out of the porthole of her luxury cabin at the wondrous vista beyond. A nearby nebula shone brightly. It was one of the unique selling points of the pleasure station. It was a sign that she was almost home.

Stretching her back, Portia looked forward to being back at the station. She had returned to Earth for three weeks so that her family could meet the little bundle peering at her with those beautiful blue eyes. The Lescal family was one of the richest in the Home System, their money and influence stretching back centuries. They owned companies and they owned governments. They ruled planets by proxy, courtesy of their financial muscle.

However, despite their money and power, nothing was as important to them as family. Family and business were inextricably linked for the Lescals. Family guaranteed continuity and continuity meant stability – and in business, continuity and stability led to success and profits. Taking the latest generation home to meet her father was the greatest gift Portia could have given her family.

'You are supposed to be sleeping,' Portia scolded her baby son affectionately. 'Are you playing tricks with me? Are you making fun of your Mummy already?'

Little Alex Lescal gurgled in reply.

Portia was so rapt, talking with her baby that she didn't notice that the view through the porthole had become static.

The *Andromedan Princess* had stopped moving.

The temple was huge and cavernous. Any sound in the temple reverberated in distorted echoes. The rocky walls were uneven with echoes deflecting from alcoves and cavern entrances hewn from the stone.

The dull murmur of a thousand devout souls at prayer came from all around the temple, though the voices are dull and low enough that it was impossible to be sure of their origin. The voices were perhaps too shrill and hollow to be human but it was impossible to be certain.

A great door creaked open and a single set of footsteps moved through the temple. With the footsteps came quiet as the murmur of the worshippers died away.

Nobody spoke when *he* was there.

His voice was rich and smooth, filled with power and a passion which spoke of absolute conviction. It was a mesmeric voice, captivating and charismatic.

None of his followers knew where he came from. He was human and his name was Vallaren but beyond that he was a mystery. That only increased the mystique surrounding him. It led to the phrase that became his legend.

He had been sent to lead them to Paradise.

Vallaren stood in the middle of the enormous temple. 'My children... my children,' he said, his voice as smooth and comforting as velvet. 'You are blessed, so blessed. This journey has been long for you. You have been asked to change so much; to sacrifice so much of yourselves. But you have done so willingly and given yourselves to a noble cause. A righteous cause.'

His congregation voiced their approval, screeching with voices that sounded like metal being torn. As Vallaren continued, the inhuman sound of monstrous voices in prayer rose in pitch and volume.

Vallaren continued, 'We have been here, isolated from the rest of the universe on our world, here on the very edge of space. But in our isolation we have grown strong. We have not been corrupted by the decadence and moral decay of the rest of the universe. Our isolation has made us strong. It has made *you* strong. And it has brought clarity to our holy cause. Our crusade. But now our time in isolation is almost over.' He paused, letting the congregation's screeches grow louder and more passionate. 'I have spent so many years with you, guiding you, shaping you for the work which lies ahead of you. Together we tested ourselves against the Venalatu system.' Again they screeched their approval. Vallaren gave them time to savour that victory before continuing. 'You have been chosen by your God for no less of a task than saving the universe and of purifying the peoples of this universe. This will not be an easy task. Sin and corruption are rooted deep in every culture, on every world. They will resist. They will fight you. But you have been made strong enough to overcome their struggles. They do not know that you are their only hope of salvation. You will take redemption to all the corners of the universe. No creature cannot be saved. You will purify them and make them fit to meet our Godhead. You are the fire of absolution.'

The temple erupted in noise. Exhorted to a frenzy by their leader, the entire assembly screamed and screeched and roared.

Vallaren stood in the middle of it all, as if absorbing the devotion and the energy of his flock. Allowing it to grow. Finally he held up his hands to dim the noise. Slowly it abated.

He waited, waited, waited, choosing his moment.

He picked every word out carefully and lingered on it. 'We... will... not... fail... our... Godhead.'

The temple was filled again with the screeching of his un-human congregation. As they screamed their raptures, Vallaren silently nodded towards the shadows where he knew an aide waited. He had given the order for the attack to begin.

The crusade was under way.

The *Andromedan Princess* shook again. Portia recognised the sound and the vibration from the countless drills and simulations they had run on the pleasure station during its refurbishment and upgrade. Those vibrations were explosive decompressions.

If the ship was decompressing, they would probably have to abandon ship. Portia scooped up her baby and hurried out into the corridor. She was met by panic and chaos. Passengers and crew milled around, looking lost and desperate for answers.

Portia grabbed a passing steward. 'What's happening?' she demanded. 'What's going on?'

'I...' the man's eyes were full of terror. Unable to answer, he pulled himself free and ran.

The voice of the ship's computer crackled over the public address speakers as if answering Portia. 'The ship is under attack,' the voice intoned flatly. 'Repeat, the ship is under attack. All passengers should make their way to the escape pods situated on deck seventeen immediately. Do not use elevators above deck seven. The hostile forces have taken this area. Repeat, all passengers should make their way to the escape pods situated on deck seventeen immediately. Do not use elevators above deck seven. Hostile forces have taken this...' the voice paused and rest. 'Correction. Hostile forces have now taken all levels above level nine.'

Portia Lescal was caught in the chaos sweeping the corridors of the *Andromedan Princess*. Passengers and crew ran in apparently random directions. All of them looked terrified and panic-stricken.

Portia cradled the back of her son's head and heald him tight against her shoulder. The crew knew this ship better than the passengers. If they were being told to head to the escape pods, they would know better than the passengers which was the fastest route. She focused her eyes on one of the domestic staff who looked after the suites on this level and followed her along the corridor at a run. Some passengers blocked her way and others simply pushed. Portia twisted her body to protect her baby son and used her shoulder to barge past the other passengers. She could have told them they were going the wrong way; told them to follow the staff... but selfishness intervened. If too many people reached the escape pods before she did then her baby would never escape. He was her first priority. Getting little Alex onto an escape pod was all that mattered.

The maid had reached a doorway up ahead and swiped her wristband across the lock. The door opened and she hurried through. An old man pushed Portia hard as he tried to get past her. She stumbled against the wall but she saw that door the maid had taken was closing. Ignoring the pain in her shoulder she forced herself forward and reached the door a fraction before it closed. The stairs beyond the door lacked the opulence of the passenger quarters but they were deserted. Looking up and down the stairwell, Portia caught sight of the maid's hand on a railing as she ran, and Portia followed her down the stairs, taking the steps as quickly as she could until finally, panting and out of breath, she reached a door marked *Deck Seventeen*. The moment she stepped through the door, Portia heard the computer's voice again.

'All passengers should make their way to the escape pods situated on deck seventeen immediately. Do not use elevators above deck thirteen. Hostile forces have now taken all levels above level thirteen.'

They were close. Whoever they were, they were close.

There were few passengers in the corridor. They all ran in the same direction as the maid. Portia realised that baby Alex was screaming. He had been screaming since she had emerged into the corridor.

'It's all right,' she tried to soothe him. 'It's going to be all right.'

Portia ran after the maid. Signs flashed on the corridor walls: **ESCAPE PODS THIS WAY**. She increased her pace, passing an older couple who were shuffling as fast as they could. She didn't stop to help them. Alex was all that mattered.

The computer voice sounded again. 'All passengers should

make their way to the escape pods situated on deck seventeen immediately. Hostile forces have now taken all levels above level sixteen. All elevators are now offline.'

Level Sixteen? They were only one level above her now. Portia kept running. And suddenly she was there. The hatches to the escape pods were on her left, set into the outer hull of the ship. Red lights shone by the first eight pods showing that they had already been ejected from the ship. A green light flashed up ahead at the ninth pod.

Hope swelled in Portia. 'Sssshh, now,' she said to the crying infant. 'It's all right, Alex. We're going to be all right.'

A huge impact shook the liner and Portia staggered, dropping to one knee.

Alex screamed all the louder. 'We're nearly there,' Portia cooed. 'We're nearly there.'

She heard footsteps from behind her in the corridor and saw a young crewman running towards her. His uniform was crimson with fresh blood. 'They've broken through. They're on this level! Even the defence robots can't hold them.'

Another hit shook the ship, this time knocking the crewman off his feet to the deck. As he scrambled to his feet, the grinding of metal gears brought a look of panic to his face. A metal shutter began to slide across the corridor.

'Hull breaches detected,' the computer crackled. 'Emergency bulkheads now being deployed.'

'No,' the crewman screamed. 'Stop it. Stop the bulkhead. Please!'

It was too late. The shutter slid into place with a solid thudding sound. Portia saw the young man's terrified face in the small Perspex window in the shutter. His terror grew more intense. He turned, looked behind him and screamed, beating his fists on the metal bulkhead and then, abruptly, he was gone, torn away from the bulkhead. A moment later, the clear panel was crimson with his blood.

Portia stared at the bloodied window in horror.

Something beyond the bulkhead moved.

A huge clawed hand began wiping the blood away.

Portia turned and ran towards the nearest escape pod. The hatches were already closing. 'No! Wait!' She saw a look of panic mixed with a silent apology on the maid's face as the escape pod closed. The green light to its side turned red and there was a slight shudder as the pod ejected in search of safety.

There was no time to be wasted on watching that. She ran to the next escape pod and punched the control to open the hatch.

The ship shook again and nearby there was the sound of rending metal.

Portia hurriedly stepped into the pod and set Alex into one of the pressure couches. The controls were simple. They had to be so that any of the passengers could operate them without training. Without checking to see if any passengers might have been approaching from the other end of the corridor, Portia slammed her hand down on the control marked LAUNCH. Hydraulic system wheezed and began to grind as the pod started its countdown in red digits on a screen.

20

19

18

The pod's hatch began to close.

17

'It's all right, Alex. We're going to be...'

Portia's words turned into a scream as claw-like hands closed on her arms and dragged her from the pod.

15

14

She twisted and stared in terror at the demon which held her shoulders.

Something else gripped her legs. Another of these monsters had her?

12

11

It was worse. The pod's hatch had closed on Portia's legs just below the knees. She felt the pressure increase. She felt her bones shatter.

The pods were for use in emergencies and were designed so that nothing would stop them from forming an air-tight seal and evacuating the stricken host vessel. The shutters simply increased pressure until they sheared through skin and muscle and shattered bone, amputating the limbs at the top of the shins.

The hatch clanged shut and the red light turned green. There was a shudder as the pod ejected.

As the darkness of unconsciousness and inevitable death from shock and blood loss wrapped itself around her, Portia Lescal was vaguely aware that her son had escaped from the ship. She was also aware that for her, there was no escape. After all, she could hardly run away now, could she? A little part of her was pleased that her last thought would be a tasteless joke but even as her vision faded, she saw the demon that had dragged her from the escape pod. She saw the blood on its mouth and the flesh clinging to its teeth.

The darkness of oblivion came as a welcome relief.

Alone in an accelerating escape pod, little Alex Lescal screamed and screamed and screamed.

Already there was no-one within a hundred kilometres to help him.

CHAPTER TWO

Andrea Hansen was in a good mood.

Actually, bollocks to that. Andy Hansen was in a *very* good mood. It was almost criminal for anyone to feel as happy as she did while they were still at work.

It had been a busy day, too. Last night there had been a disco at the Students' Union. It had been a proper disco, too, themed to the 1970s and everybody had to dress appropriately.

The university specialised in history and had a museum attached. Andy ran on-site the café which serviced both establishments and regularly attended social events there even though she wasn't a student... yet.

That one word was part of the reason she was so happy. Being a café manager had paid the bills after her parents had died but it hadn't been her career plan. She had always wanted to go to university to study. Well, now that was going to happen and she was going to be starting at *this* university after summer. Andy had no doubt that strings had been pulled for her to be accepted. The fact that the museum's curator was one of her closest friends really counted for something. Being friends with the vice chancellor and having her bacon, egg and black pudding roll ready for her arrival every Friday morning didn't hurt either.

Part of Andy's brain rebelled at the thought of giving up work and going back to education. She had grown used to seeing money go into her bank account every month.

What she hadn't grown used to was the knowledge that she didn't have to worry about money anymore. And she certainly couldn't explain to most people *why* she didn't have to worry about money.

Who knew time travel would be so useful for her finances?

Travelling to distant planets galaxies was all fine and tickety-boo but she still had to pay bills at home. Travelling in time, opening accounts in the past, making regular deposits at various intervening points meant that Andy now had a very healthy seven or eight figure bank account, thank you very much, and she didn't actually *need* to work.

Except that she did. Andy was never going to be content doing nothing. It just wasn't her. It wasn't how her friends worked either. They all had to be busy, to be doing something, preferably something useful.

Those friends were now sitting at a table in Andy's café, while she started getting ready to close for the day. After last night's disco – at which she had looked *absolutely fabulous darling*, in a red one piece jumpsuit – the students had kept the café busy with a constant demand for hangover-salving bacon rolls, fried egg rolls, and anything-else-you-can-fit-on-a-roll rolls. It had been a really good day, laughing with those students after a really good night laughing with those students and partying with her friends.

Normally there would only have been Ibrahim, the curator of the museum, and Erimem waiting for her. She wouldn't even begin to try to explain Erimem. How do you explain that your best friend is a time travelling ex-Pharaoh who could kick the crap out of Hulk Hogan without trying even though she was hardly over five feet tall, but who was also borderline addicted to the BBC's daytime drama *Doctors* and a full-on chocolate addict and after last night, a disco diva – how could she explain all of that without being carted away. She just didn't try.

Today was not a normal day. Helena, Ibrahim's wife was sitting with Ibrahim and Erimem, as was Olivia.

Olivia.

Yeah, Olivia was hard to explain, too. Explaining that her girlfriend was actually a twenty year old pirate captain from three hundred years ago was as likely to get her a lovely hug-me straightjacket and a trip to the local home for the terminally bewildered.

What made things easier was that there were no real secrets

among those four. Well, there were some bed-time shenanigans
that she and Olivia were keeping to themselves and Ibrahim and
Helena were probably the same, but in all the important things,
they were a family and they all knew each other's secrets.

All except the last and most recent addition to the party. He
was tall, a bit over six feet and around thirty with dark hair that
desperately wanted to be untidy but which he just about managed
to tame. He wore a suit but had the shirt's top button undone and
the tie pulled loose.

He was Detective Sergeant Adam Docherty – and he fancied
Erimem something rotten.

That didn't bother Andy at all. Adam was a good guy. There
had been a number of disappearances at the university just after
Erimem had arrived – a large number of the faculty had gone
missing. One of the secrets Adam didn't know was that those
faculty members had been a demon-worshipping, Armageddon-
embracing time-travelling cult who had tried to kill this friendly
little group. They had succeeded in killing a number of the
students as blood sacrifices. In the end, Erimem had led her new
band of friends to beat – and kill – the cult members. Given that
Adam was the police officer who had been assigned to look after
things at the university it was probably best that he didn't know
about any of that or he would probably have to arrest them all.
And Andy could think of a more fun way to use handcuffs.
Actually, Olivia didn't know about how close they had come to
dying at the hands of that cult either. That had been a year or
more before Andy had met her. At least relatively speaking, for
her it had been eighteen months. In calendar terms... three
hundred plus years had passed. Time travel really was a bugger
for keeping track of the time.

Andy saw Adam and Erimem laugh at something. Yep, he
fancied her something rotten and though she wouldn't admit it,
her best friend fancied the pants off DS Adam Docherty. It was
probably the accent. Everybody knew Scottish accents were
sexy. Even Andy had to admit there was something about that
Edinburgh accent. She wondered how Adam would react if he
found out that Erimem had been born almost three and a half
millennia ago. Well, that wasn't a conversation she would have
to have. That was Erimem's task if and when she chose to take

it on. For now all five of them were laughing and that was a great thing to see.

Helena noticed that Andy was looking in their direction and discretely tapped her watch. Andy got the message and glanced at the clock. That was it. One minute to closing time.

Her heart sank as the café door opened. What twat would actually come in at this time of day?

She saw who it was. Oh, it was *that* twat.

Tom Niven was not her favourite person. In fact, when she had started working in the café she had quickly come to hate him. He was an entitled prick from a wealthy old American family, and he had developed a reputation in his first two years for living by his "Three Fs" philosophy – find 'em, fuck 'em, forget 'em. He must have worked his way through an unhealthily high percentage of the female students in those years and when a girl wouldn't sleep with him he just lied and said she did.

That was why Andy had come to hate him.

Coming out isn't easy, not even in somewhere as cosmopolitan as a London university in the Twenty First Century. Andy had still been on those early, baby steps of her first relationship with another woman when Tom had blundered his nose into her life. Sasha was from Ukraine, five feet six, with long black hair and the most hypnotic hazel eyes set in the most gorgeous face. Andy had fallen hard and Sasha had caught her. They had quietly gone about their relationship for two months, keeping it entirely private. That was as much for Sasha's sake as for Andy's. Sasha didn't come from what could be called a progressive family. Her father had been against her going to university. He thought she should work in an office then get married and have children. Her mother thought the same but with added visits to church every Sunday and prayers every night. That wasn't the ideal environment for her to discover that she was an atheist and a lesbian. London should have been great for her except that one of her cousins was also at the uni, and he was a dick. One night in the Union, Tom Niven had come on hard to Sasha. He hadn't taken the subtle hints that she wasn't interested and he hadn't paid much attention to being told flat out to "fuck off and die". Instead, the next day he had spread the story that he had slept with Sasha and that she had been "one dirty bitch".

Those three words had followed Sasha for a month. She couldn't explain that when she was supposed to be in bed with Tom Niven she had actually been in bed with her girlfriend, Andy. There had been plenty of sex involved but Tom Niven hadn't. No matter how Sasha protested it wasn't true, Tom just repeated the claim, his revenge for being rejected. Eventually the story made its way to Sasha's cousin and suddenly her parents were on the phone demanding that she return to Ukraine in disgrace. In the end she had transferred to Edinburgh, far from Tom Niven and his lies but also far from Andy. They had talked of travelling to meet, of making the long-distance relationship work... but it had only been talk. The death of their relationship had broken Andy's heart, and she blamed Tom Niven for it. Unfortunately Tom had been one of the people dragged into Erimem's orbit by the time travelling cult. His latest conquest, Anna, had been killed by them in Ancient Greece. Tom had never quite recovered from it. He had, for the most part, retreated into his studies and worked at his degree, and had recently signed up for another two years. While their experiences had brought the rest of the group closer – as close as family – it had the opposite effect on Tom. He was an only child and it appeared that he never saw either of his parents. They were divorced and neither had time for him. He didn't seem to know what to do. He couldn't get past his responsibility for Anna's death but he wasn't close enough to his parents to talk to them. He was stuck. That was probably why he had opted for two more years at university. While he usually avoided Andy or Erimem or Ibrahim for the guilty memories they would provoke, the university was the one secure and solid thing in his life.

What pissed Andy off was that she now felt sorry for the shit who had been responsible for her heart being broken. Having Olivia in her life was probably part of that. She was happy and she was in love. That made it easier to forgive and forget. Well, maybe not forget. And maybe not forgive either, but at least she was over it. Whatever was eating Tom still had its teeth buried into him.

Andy forced a semblance of a smile onto her face. 'What can I get you?'

Tom looked dully at the counter, as if he hadn't expected the question. 'Oh, you're closing up.' He plucked a can of Diet Fanta from the fridge. 'I'll just have this, please, Andy.'

Andy scanned the can, took Tom's money and handed over the change. 'Here you go.' She felt that she should say something more given everything that they had shared. 'So, how have you been?'

'Busy,' he answered. He wasn't the same arrogant, cocky little prick she can come to loathe. He was quiet and insecure, almost afraid to just be there.

'Hi, Tom.' Ibrahim's voice startled Tom and he turned towards the table.

'Oh, hi,' Tom answered. He looked edgy but forced a smile to accompany his reply.

'How have you been?' Helena asked.

Tom's answer was unconvincing. 'I'm okay.' He sounded anything but okay.

As a doctor, Helena was the one of the group perhaps most disposed to be open to Tom. More than once she had suggested that he seek counselling to deal with his trauma. While he wasn't her patient she had been clear that he needed to be *somebody's* patient.

'Sit down,' Helena said, indicating a spare chair at the table that had been occupied by Andy just a few minutes earlier.

Tom crossed to the table but didn't sit. 'I shouldn't stay,' he said. 'I don't want to intrude.'

Helena's expression was unusually serious. 'Don't be silly. Sit.' She tapped the chair with her foot.

Tom still looked uncertain but he sat. 'Thanks.'

Helena was obviously keen to push the discussion. 'So, how have you been keeping? Are you sleeping all right?'

'Not really,' Tom admitted. 'Not since... well, you know.'

'Still?' Helena asked. 'What about Christmas? Did you go home?'

Tom shook his head. 'No. Mom was busy and Dad... well, he had something on again.'

'You should have come across to our place,' Ibrahim said.

Andy saw Erimem's eyebrow twitch at that suggestion. Apparently nobody else did.

'I thought you might be, you know, *away*,' Tom said.

'No,' Helena answered, 'a quiet Christmas at home.' She eyed Tom carefully. 'I think you could probably do with getting away to somewhere nice and relaxing, though. You know what I mean?'

'Yes.'

Helena nodded to herself. 'As a doctor, I'm recommending it. Talk to Ibrahim about it tomorrow – and don't make him come looking for you.'

'Okay.' The relief in Tom's voice was palpable. He hefted his can of juice. 'Look, I probably should get back to my dissertation.' He looked gratefully at both Helena and Ibrahim. 'Thanks. I mean it.'

'See you tomorrow,' Ibrahim said.

Tom nodded. 'Tomorrow.' With that he hurried towards the door.

As the door closed, Andy flopped into the chair Tom had vacated.

'Finished?' Olivia asked eagerly.

Andy's head bobbed in agreement. 'All done,' she confirmed, looking around the little group. 'So what are the plans for tonight?'

Helena stifled a yawn. 'After last night's shenanigans at the disco, it's home, dinner, a movie and then an early night.' She shrugged. 'I'm *very* old, remember. I can't party two school nights in a row.'

Adam gave a snort of laughter. 'You're not old,' he said. 'I can only be a few years younger than you.'

Smirks and grins were suppressed. Adam was the only one not in on everybody else's secrets. Erimem would have to know him a lot better before the topic of time travel was broached with him.

Helena settled for scrunching her nose and nudging Ibrahim. 'See? Somebody here is a gentleman.' She gave a slight bow to Adam. 'Thank you, kind sir.'

'I think,' Erimem said carefully, 'that we are mature, not old.'

Helena tapped the table with a finger. 'On the nosey!'

'Ooh,' Erimem bounced in her seat with excitement. 'I know that reference. *Young Frankenstein*.' She sounded very pleased with herself.

'One of my favourite films,' Adam said.

'And mine,' Erimem agreed. 'I like black and white films.'

Andy held back from mentioning that Erimem's fondness for black and white might because she had appeared in three cheapo black and white films back in the 1940s... and they would have to travel back in time soon to make the second of the movies or history would get very cranky.

'So,' Andy said, 'pizza and a black and white classic?'

Adam sighed. 'You're making me jealous. I'm on duty tonight.' He glanced at his watch. 'Starting in about twenty minutes.' He looked over at Ibrahim. 'The security on your new exhibits is perfect. I'll email you across confirmation by morning.'

Ibrahim gave a thumbs up. 'Great. That will get the insurance company and the vice chancellor's assistant off my back. Thanks.'

'No worries.' Adam pushed his seat back and stood. 'Thanks for the coffee and the company.'

Andy tipped an imaginary hat. 'Pleasure.'

'Okay,' Adam said, 'I'd better make a move.' He gave a little wave. 'See you all later.'

Nobody missed that as he said goodbye, his eyes lingered with Erimem the longest.

'Oh, for God's sake just snog the man,' Andy said as the door closed behind Adam.

'What are you talking about?' Erimem objected innocently.

Helena just gave her a look.

'He is a very nice young man,' Olivia said with approval. 'Although,' she added, 'I don't know how to judge men. The one I was engaged to turned out to be a murderous scoundrel pirate.' She shrugged. 'Besides, I am only attracted to women.'

'*Woman*,' Andy corrected. 'You are only attracted to one woman.' She smiled cheesily. 'You can even name names if you want, as long as it's me.'

Olivia answered by poking her tongue out cheekily.

Ibrahim raised his hands in surrender. 'I am not getting involved in this conversation. It would not be appropriate for me to give dating advice to my many-times great aunt.'

'At last,' Erimem sighed, 'one of you I can listen to.'

'But he *does* have the hots for you,' Ibrahim added.
Erimem slumped over the table. 'I despise all of you.'
Everyone else just smiled.

CHAPTER THREE

The starcruiser *Saint-Saens* cut effortlessly through space. Though it was a ship that would never enter or leave a planet's atmosphere, having been built in orbit around Mars at the Phobos shipyard and docks, the *Saint-Saens* was actually a sleek and elegant spaceship. It benefitted from having been designed and constructed during a period in Earth's history where art and culture were respected and revered. A spaceship like the *Saint-Saens* could as easily and efficiently have been a square or the shape of a brick. But current sensibilities would not allow that. It didn't just have to operate like a deadly warship capable of high faster-than-light speeds, it had to look fast and look like a warship, too. It was an era when aesthetics mattered. And the *Saint-Saens* was a beautiful-looking warship. Someone at the shipyard had suggested that anyone facing the *Saint-Saens* in battle would want to take its picture before the battle started. That person was soundly decried as an idiot who had never seen battle, but that didn't diminish the fact that the *Saint-Saens* was a beautiful ship.

The command deck – the bridge – of the *Saint-Saens* was a mixture of gleaming white and steel grey with the only flashes of colour coming from the display panels in front of the crew members seated at their stations.

First Officer Rebecca Lee sat in the centre of the rectangular room, in the captain's chair. She was of average height and on the athletic side of slim. Her black hair was neatly trimmed to shoulder length, framing a rather beautiful face which suggested an Asian ancestry. She was recording an update into the ship's log.

'Now leaving Sector Fourteen and entering Sector Fifteen, the *Saint-Saens* is on schedule for interception.'

She pressed the pause button to halt recording at the doors to the side of the bridge slid open. She eased up from the command chair and turned to face the newcomer to the bridge.

'Captain Watson,' she said.

Barnaby Watson smiled at his first officer. She didn't return the smile. She never did, but he had learned not to take it personally. Lee just wasn't built for shows of emotion. 'What's our status, Mr Lee?' he asked, adhering to the old naval tradition of calling every crewman "Mister". It was one of the habits he had tried to impose on his ship to remind the crew of their links to seafaring mariners of past centuries. These traditions mattered to Watson. They brought order and security to the running of a ship. On top of that, he just *liked* them. He liked the atmosphere they brought to a ship.

As ever, Commander Lee answered efficiently. That was not surprising. She was known to be one of the most competent officers serving in the fleet. 'On schedule, Captain,' she answered in a level tone. 'We should be in scanning range of the *Andromedan Princess* in approximately three minutes.'

Watson was sure that Lee would know to the second how far they were from scanning range of the stricken liner but she would have deliberately rounded off the time to appear a little less than she was, to fit in with the crew around her. She was dumbing herself down so he wouldn't feel intimidated. He was both grateful for her thoughtfulness and viciously angry at her arrogance in thinking she had to slow down for him.

His real irritation came from knowing that she was right.

The captain nodded, accepting the report. 'That's if the ship's still in one piece. Before the radio cut out, her reports said she took a hell of a beating.'

He could almost see running the schematics of the liner through her memory. 'The *Andromedan Princess* is a Barcelona class ship, sir,' she said. 'One of the sturdiest design of passenger ships in service.'

That was true. Watson had travelled on a Barcelona class ship once. He had been deployed to an outpost and the liner was the only ship passing nearby. To the immense annoyance of many of his colleagues Watson had been forced to endure five days of First Class luxury. A self-confessed geek for anything related to space travel, Watson had spent a good part of each day with the engineering and technical crews learning about the ship. He had been impressed enough to recommend that in times of war, the Barcelona class ships could be commandeered and turned into troop carriers.

But even the sturdiest of ships could only take so much beating.

'Well,' Watson said, 'let's hope she's still there. Anything from Command Central?'

As expected, Lee reported instantly. 'Seven more life pods have been tracked to a nearby planet, sir. Forty-two expected survivors in total.'

Forty two? Was that all? They couldn't contain a fraction of the crew and passengers from the *Andromedan Princess*. He couldn't show despair to the crew, though. They didn't need to ever see that from their captain. He had to exude calm and reassurance. 'That's something, at least,' he said.

Even Worsely didn't think he sounded in any way convincing.

Lee wasn't finished with her report. 'Command also reports that they found the remains of at least sixteen of the *Andromedan Princess*'s life pods,' she continued. 'The wreckage was so badly damaged they are having difficulty working out exactly how many pods they've found. Or how many dead bodies.'

That level of destruction visited upon so many escape pods pointed to one unpleasant conclusion. It made Watson's mouth go dry. 'Good God. They even shot the escape pods.'

'It looks that way, sir,' Lee agreed.

Watson felt the weight on his shoulders grow just a bit heavier and an angry tightness grip his heart a little harder. 'Captain Lescal's sister and the baby?'

'No sign of them in either the survivors or casualties lists,' Lee replied without the need to check her data, 'but we're still genetically sifting a lot of the recovered biomatter – and a large number of the pods are still unaccounted for.'

That was not what Watson had been hoping to hear. It had

been a long shot and mathematically unlikely that Lescal's sister or nephew would be in the small percentage who had survived. Still, it was a kick in the stomach to know they hadn't been found. 'You'd better tell her to get ready,' he told Lee. 'I assume she'll want to come with us when we board the liner.'

Lee was already keying instructions into her pad, electronically issuing orders for troops to prepare to move in full battle readiness. 'She's already prepared, sir,' Lee replied. 'Captain Lescal called up a few minutes ago.'

Normally that would have pushed Watson into a fury. A visiting captain, especially one from another service, should not simply contact his bridge to badger his officers. But in this case, he understood the reasoning. 'I'm not happy having the army muscle in on Fleet business like this, Lee,' he said, 'but it's family. I'd do the same myself.'

Lee nodded with a curiously detached expression. 'I'm sure you're right, sir. I'm unlikely to ever find out for myself.'

'What?' Worley frowned for just a moment then shook himself. How could he be stupid enough to forget who and what Commander Lee was? 'Oh, I keep forgetting you're an android, Lee.' He grimaced. 'Sorry. And I'm not allowed to call you an android these days, am I?'

An almost human smile of reassurance tugged at the corners of Lees' mouth. 'I don't mind, captain, but I believe the currently acceptable term is Synth. Synthetic life-form.'

Watson cursed his own stupidity. He had been warned by Fleet Command about using insensitive terminology in front of the andr... in front of the Synths. Times were changing with the Synths getting full citizenship rights and the Fleet Command was cracking down on older officers who couldn't adapt to the changing universe around them. He had no intention of allowing a slip of the tongue to wash his career out of the airlock. 'Right,' he said to Lee, 'Synths it is.'

'At least you didn't call me a "glorified toaster",' sir,' Lee said wryly.

Well, Watson didn't have to ask who would have said that to his XO. Their army guest had made no secret of her distaste for Synths since coming aboard. 'Having trouble with Captain Lescal again?' he said. 'I'll have a word with her. She'll get the full riot act this time.'

Lee shook her head quickly causing her black hair to shimmer. 'It doesn't matter, sir. The worry about her sister is bound to be affecting her.'

As usual, Lee had a point. 'Probably,' Watson conceded. 'You're a good person, Lee. Well, a good andr... Synth.' He puffed his cheeks and exhaled in exasperation. 'You know what I mean.'

'I think so,' Lee replied, an unusual tone of what sounded like pride in her voice. 'Thank you. I have a small boarding party prepared.'

'Full arms?' Watson asked. He didn't want his troops going in unless they were ready for a fight.

'Heavy weapons,' Lee assured him. 'Just in case things get...' she sought the right word, '...tetchy.'

Heavy weapons made sense. They were for use in a war zone. The reports sent back from the *Andromedan Princess* – and now from another outpost – were clear that a war zone was exactly what they were likely to find. Watson accepted Lee's actions but added an extra order of his own. 'Break out an extra set of heavy weapons. I think I'll join you.'

As expected, Lee protested. 'Captain...'

Watson had prepared his argument and interrupted his first officer. 'I know it's against regs for us both to go, but my mind's made up.'

Every other Synth Watson knew would have argued further. Lee simply nodded her acceptance. 'You're the captain, sir.'

The chirp of a control interrupted the conversation and Lee immediately crossed to a panel. She reads the display quickly. 'We've detected the *Andromedan Princess*,' she said. 'We're in scanner range.'

Watson hurried to a position from which he would have a better view of the main viewer screen. 'Show me. Let's see her.'

'Yes, sir.' Lee operated controls on her command panel and the starscape on the screen changed to show the brutalised body of the *Andomedan Princess*.

'Dear lord,' Watson breathed, looking at the ship in horror.

Lee had moved to his shoulder. 'It's amazing she's still intact.'

It did seem miraculous that the ship hadn't disintegrated. Vicious gouges along her hull opened through the multiple bulkheads into the interior of the ship. Through some portholes, fires could be seen burning while lights flickered unsteadily in other windows as the power fluctuated wildly. Weapons fire had left angry black char-marks on the ship's once pristine hull and a gas of some kind was venting from a conduit in its side, putting the ship into a lazy spin.

Watson forced himself to concentrate. He had a job to do. 'Atmosphere?' he asked.

Lee returned to her control panels and read the results of her scans. 'Hull integrity is secure in most places,' she said. 'The atmosphere is mostly breathable.'

That was better than Watson had expected. 'Take us alongside and deploy docking tube.'

'Yes, sir,' Lee said, relaying the order to the ship's navigator.

The ship slowed and began manoeuvring towards the ailing liner.

Tom Niven had surprised everyone – apparently including himself – by actually turning up to meet Ibrahim as he had promised. He remained as skittish and on edge as he had been the previous day but at least he had kept the appointment.

Helena had suggested that Ibrahim be the one Tom meet because she was sure that on some level Tom felt a closer affinity with her husband than with any of the others. 'It might be because they're both men,' she had said. 'It might be because they went through that first experience together in Ancient Greece and it almost killed Ibrahim, too. Or,' she had shrugged, 'it might be because he's scared of women who possess both breasts and the ability to tell him an opinion he doesn't want to hear.'

'My opinions he can have,' Andy had answered. 'The bazooms are off limits.'

The odd thing was that for someone who had been so led by his groin, Tom had barely been seen in the company of a girl for months, maybe years. It hadn't been something they had thought about because Tom hadn't been something they had thought about.

There had been a good deal of guilt about that. While they had been living their lives, Tom had been drowning in his.

Helena in particular had felt that she had failed him. 'I'm a doctor. It's my job to look after people. I didn't do much of a job with him. He needed help and he still does.'

'Meaning?' That was asked by Andy.

Helena had a plan in mind. It was quite simply to take Tom away through time and space to somewhere relaxing and to get him talking – and to find a way to start moving him past his trauma.

Ibrahim and Erimem had been given the task of suggesting the plan to Tom, with Helena coming in later to add weight to the argument. As it transpired, Tom leaped at the chance to get away from his everyday life. There was something almost pitiful in the way he thanked them over and over.

It was a Friday and the obvious time to take Tom away. Olivia's visit to the Twenty First Century was hardly an obstacle to them going away to a distant world in search of relaxation and pampering. While she had been an inexperienced and rather insular when she had met Andy, the last few years had opened her eyes not only to the possibilities of her own world but to the wonders of other times and places. On her first visit to Andy's home time period Olivia had screamed and panicked and begged to be taken back to her own era. Now she was finding the restrictions of her own time painfully limiting and she was spending more and more of her time in Twenty First Century London. Both she and Andy were aware that they were close to reaching the point at which a decision on their future as a couple would have to be made. Going public at Helena and Ibrahim's wedding had moved them into serious territory. But for now, they had been looking forward to a weekend – which could easily become a fortnight – away together and with friends.

The only vaguely dissenting voices about Tom joining the trip were Andy and Erimem. They were both sympathetic and they both saw the sense of it, but there was something about him that made them both uneasy. They were both convinced it had to do with his previous unreliable and often vicious behaviour. In the end, Erimem had simply said, 'If he is to change then perhaps so must we.'

She had, however, made one stipulation. Tom was not to know where the entrance to her Habitat was.

While Erimem called her Habitat "home", Andy had other names for it, most regularly "Narnia". In the first adventure that had so badly scarred Tom, Erimem had obtained what Andy rightly called "a world of her own". The Habitat was a self-contained artificial universe which she accessed through a portal which could be made to look like any kind of doorway she chose. At the moment it looked very much like a linen cupboard located on the upstairs landing of Helena and Ibrahim's house.

Erimem didn't want Tom to know that. He simply wasn't part of their little circle of friends and he wasn't allowed to know something so secret. Instead he would meet them in the canteen and use the travel rings to transport directly into the Habitat. The excuse given to Tom was that it would save time and he had accepted that willingly.

The party began to assemble in the canteen at just before five o'clock. The students had long since stopped work for the week and made a bee-line to the Union or to any one of the local boozers but as faculty, Ibrahim had to work until five, and as she was technically employed as his assistant, so did Erimem. If the faculty were still on duty, so was the canteen, which meant Andy was just putting of the last of the perishables into the fridge and freezer when Ibrahim and Erimem wandered in.

'Hi,' Andy waved.

Erimem bounced across to the counter. 'Is it too late to ask for a bacon roll?'

'Yes,' Andy answered, 'and you only asked to annoy me, so you can sod off.' She grinned. 'And with the pleasantries out of the way...' She closed the fridge, made sure the cash was locked away, came out from behind the counter and gave her friend a hug. 'I am *so* looking forward to getting away for a bit.'

The door opened but they were surprised that it wasn't Tom who entered. Helena and Olivia came in.

'Surprise!' Helena said.

Ibrahim kissed her quickly. 'A bit, but a good surprise.'

'I thought we should all go to the Habitat together,' Helena said.

Erimem had overheard the conversation and nodded her agreement. 'That will make him feel more included.'

Andy and Olivia took a little longer over kissing their hello. A couple of years earlier Andy would never have been confident enough to show that kind of affection for a girlfriend. She was considerably more surprised by how quickly Olivia had grasped the freedom to express herself that was afforded in the Twenty First Century.

'Nice hello,' Andy said.

'I know,' Olivia smiled back. 'I don't say hello to everyone that way.'

'I'm glad to hear it.'

They were distracted as the door opened again. Tom entered carrying a rucksack. 'Hi,' he said. 'Sorry if I'm late.'

'You're not,' Helena reassured him, 'but you've been in Britain so long you've picked up the habit of apologising for things you haven't done. Congratulations. You're fitting in.'

He answered with a half-smile. 'I guess I have been here a while now.'

'Shall we go?' Helena asked. 'We should get this show on the road. I have something for you, Tom.' She fished a time travel ring from her pocket.

And so did Erimem. 'So do I.' She shrugged and slipped the ring back into her pocket.

'Great minds think alike,' Helena smiled. She passed the ring to Tom, who gave a slight wince at the piece of jewellery bonded itself to him. 'I forgot it hurts,' he said.

Erimem lifted her thumb, on which she always wore her travel ring. 'Why do you think I never take mine off?'

Andy pulled her keys out of a pocket and swung them like an old movie gunslinger. 'You guys head back. I'll lock the door and follow.'

'I'll wait with you,' Erimem said.

Andy's nose wrinkled. 'You're a pal.'

'I know.'

'Remember the drill?' Helena asked Tom. 'Just twist the ring.'

Tom nodded. 'I remember.'

'Okay,' Helena said. 'Now.'

Ibrahim, Helena, Tom and Olivia twisted their travel rings and were engulfed in a ball of spitting, roiling electricity. The last thing they saw before the electricity faded was Olivia blowing a kiss to Andy.

'Okay,' Andy said, 'time to lock up.' She stopped, staring at the door. 'Oh, bollocks.'

Erimem turned and also saw the open door. 'Yes,' she said. 'Bollocks.'

Standing in the doorways, his mouth slack with shock, was Detective Sergeant Adam Docherty.

CHAPTER FOUR

'There's an explanation for that,' Adam Docherty said. His voice sounded unusually dull. 'I'm buggered if I know what it is but there has to be an explanation for that.'

'Kind of depends what "that" is,' Andy said slowly.

Erimem nodded. 'What did you see?'

'Nothing,' Adam answered. 'Nothing... well, four people fading into nothing.'

Erimem's shoulders slumped. 'Would you believe it was a trick of the light?'

'No.'

'Don't blame you,' Andy said, 'it was a shit excuse.' She grimaced at Erimem. 'Sorry, pal, but it was.'

'I know,' Erimem agreed miserably, 'but it was the best I could think of.'

'So where are they?' Adam demanded. He seemed to have found his composure and his policeman's manner. 'What happened to them?'

'Nothing *happened* to them,' Erimem answered.

'She's right,' Andy agreed. 'They're fine, and probably wondering what's happened to us.'

'Shall we phone them and find out?' Adam challenged.

Andy nudged Erimem. 'I think we have to come clean, kid.'

Erimem nodded and pursed her lips in a petulant pout. 'You are right,' she said. She didn't sound happy but pulled the spare travel ring from her pocket and handed it to Adam. 'Put this on and do as I instruct you.'

Andy knew that tone well enough. 'Best do as she tells you.'

She eased Adam inside and locked the door. 'She's a Pharaoh. She's used to getting her own way.'

'What?' Confusion disappeared as Adam slid the ring on and winced as it bonded to him.

'We should have warned you about that,' Erimem said. 'Sorry.'

'Our bad,' Andy agreed.

'Now,' said Erimem, 'twist the central band of the ring.'

'Where are they?' Ibrahim grumbled impatiently.

The four who had travelled back to the Habitat had gathered their luggage and were ready to head off to what Helena promised was "the most tranquil spot in the nine galaxies", at least according to the Habitat's computer. Tom was the only one who had drifted away, and was looking in awe at the herd of Woolly Mammoths ambling across the vast grass expanse beyond the terrace outside of Erimem's quite beautiful villa.

'Just locking up,' Helena said. 'Calm down. There's nothing to worry about.' She saw three figures come through from the transport room and her shoulders slumped. 'Oh, what do I know?'

'What happened?' Adam asked. 'Where are we? What is this place?'

'This is my home,' Erimem explained. 'This is where I live. Or at least where I sleep and relax.'

'And have parties,' Olivia added.

That was certainly true. 'Yes,' Erimem agreed with a little smile. 'And sometimes I have wonderful parties here.'

'But where is here?' Adam demanded. 'That doesn't look like the University outside.' He hurried to the large glass sliding doors to the terrace and stopped, staring at the giant hairy – and supposedly extinct – animals outside. 'Those are...'

'You poor sod,' Ibrahim said sympathetically. 'You have a lot to take in.'

'Yes,' Erimem agreed, 'we have a great deal to talk about.'

'Then why don't we do it somewhere lovely?' Helena asked brightly. 'I'm sure you'd find this easier in a more relaxing situation. We'll have the Habitat rustle up something for Adam to wear and when we get where we're going, you two can have your chat.'

'Long chat,' Andy said. 'Long, long, long chat.'

Erimem's reply was most un-Pharaoh-like. 'Oh, shut *uuuup*,'

'This is Commander Lee of the Earth Cruiser *Saint-Saens* to any survivors on the *Andromedan Princess*. We are moving into docking position.' The PA system on board the *Andromedan Princess* crackled, trying to relay the incoming message from the warship. 'This is Commander Lee of the Earth Cruiser *Saint-Saens* to any survivors on the *Andromedan Princess*. We are moving into docking position.'

The dull emergency lights flickered, dimmed and returned to their usual gloomy reddish hue. White noise hissed from some flaw in the communications, and somewhere a fluid pipeline had ruptured causing a constant *drip-drip-drip*.

The ominous atmosphere was shattered by a crackling, spitting ball of electricity which deposited seven figures into a corridor.

Helena looked around the dull corridor in confusion. 'And this is... not the Eye of Wherever-it-is, I'd guess.'

Andy shared the confusion and disappointment. Her navigation skills with the time travel apparatus had never let her down before. Well, not recently and not this badly. 'Er, not as such, no.'

Olivia caught Andy's hand. 'So by "not as such", you mean...'

Andy grimaced. 'Not at all?'

'Are we even close?' Ibrahim asked.

Andy tried to bluster it out. 'Cosmically speaking? In the great scheme of things? Considering the near infinite nature of time and space and the...'

'You haven't got a clue, where we are, have you?' Erimem said.

Andy sighed. 'Not so's you'd notice. No.' She moved to a porthole and looked out. 'But I can honestly say we're in space. That's a start.'

Even in the dull light, Adam Docherty visibly paled. 'We're

where?'

Ibrahim placed a friendly hand on his shoulder. 'You've been thrown in at the deep end,' he said sympathetically. 'You'll get used to it.'

Adam swallowed hard. 'I'm really hoping we're still at the 70s disco and I'm just on one wild high from a hash brownie or something.'

'Sorry,' Ibrahim said. 'This is real.'

Andy had found a computer display panel on the wall and was coaxing some life into it. The screen flickered and crackled. 'Bingo!' she exclaimed, quickly running her eyes across the juddering display. 'We are on the *Andromedan Princess*,' she reported. 'Apparently it's a space liner.'

'Another liner?' Helena was thoroughly disappointed. 'I hope there's less trouble than last time.' She offered Tom an apologetic glance. 'Sorry about this. It's not quite what we had planned for you.'

'It's fine,' Tom said, looking around worried. He was terrible at hiding how nervous he was.

'What happened to this ship?' Erimem asked.

That was typical of her, thought Andy. Whenever there was a problem she slipped into the pragmatic, problem-solving mode. 'I can't find that information. The computer's goosed. At least this terminal is.'

'We should find the command deck of this ship,' Erimem said. 'Andy, can you find it?'

'Or we can just go back to London and you all tell me what the hell is going on,' Adam blurted out.

Erimem turned to Adam. This wasn't part of herself that she had shown him before. This was what Andy sometimes termed her Pharaoh-face. When trouble surfaced, Erimem simply moved towards practical solutions to the problems, and that meant that she automatically took charge. It was just part of her make-up.

'You have many questions,' Erimem said to Adam, 'and I will answer them. However, we are currently on a ship which is badly damaged and we have seen no people. They may be hurt, they might need our help. I will answer your questions later.'

She turned and went back to Andy. 'The command deck?'

41

Andy poked a finger towards a duller part of the corridor. 'That way. Eleven decks up. Stairs only, the lifts are off.'

The lights on the stairs were even duller than in the corridor. The emergency lights flickered uncertainly.

'Everyone stay together,' Erimem called. She had made her way to the front of the group.

'If there's a chance of survivors, shouldn't we split up and search?' Andy asked.

'No.' Erimem's voice was colder than usual. Quiet but cold. Logical. 'We stay together. I don't think we will find many survivors.'

Helena had spotted the change in Erimem as well. 'Why not?'

The harsh white of the light on Erimem's mobile phone flared in the stairwell. The cream wall ahead was splattered with a crimson that had almost dried to brown.

'Shit,' Helena said.

'I was sure I could smell blood,' Erimem said. She pointed at the pattern of blood on the wall. 'This is violent.'

Helena agreed. 'It's like the spray from multiple blades.'

Tom sounded terrified. 'Whoever did this – how do we know they're not still here?'

Andy had asked herself the same question and hadn't liked the answer. 'We don't.'

Erimem looked back, as if she was remembering Tom was there for the first time. 'Tom, if you wish to go back to the Habitat, do so. It will definitely be safer. You should think of this also, Adam.'

Surprisingly it was Tom who answered. 'No,' he said. 'I'll stay. I'm no use to anybody if I run away again.'

Adam shrugged. 'Looks like I'll have to stay as well, then.'

Erimem was already moving up the stairs, aiming her phone's torch upwards. 'As you wish. Stay close and move fast.'

The rest of the stairwell and the corridors leading to the liner's bridge were all abandoned and sprayed with blood. The flight deck itself showed signs of having been the location of a brutal firefight. Blaster marks signed walls and computers consoles, but they were largely obscured by drying blood.

'They put up a fight anyway,' Andy said.

Ibrahim agreed but was distracted by the amount of blood coating the controls. 'Yes, but they still lost.'

'Then where are they?' Erimem asked. 'The bodies. Where are they?'

Helena ran a hand through her thick, curly hair. 'That's a fair point. Blood loss like this means dead bodies. Nobody is surviving that kind of trauma.'

'And the ship is abandoned,' Erimem added. 'Derelict, even. Why would they tidy the bodies away?'

The answer was obvious, to some of the party at least. Andy saw the understanding in Ibrahim and Helena's faces. 'They've got a use for the bodies.'

'What kind of use?' Olivia asked. A second later realisation dawned and she screwed up her face. 'Oh. No.'

Andy squeezed Olivia's hand reassuringly.

Erimem's focus was on the task at hand rather than her friends' concerns. 'Andy, can you make sense of these controls?' she asked. 'It would be useful if we could get enough power to access the memory and perhaps shipboard cameras.'

'Do you want me to rustle up peace in the Middle East while I'm at it?' Andy asked sarcastically. 'Maybe catch Jack the Ripper if I've got a minute to spare? Explain all seven seasons of *Game of Thrones* to somebody who's never seen it?'

'Just the power for now,' Erimem said, almost ignoring the sarcasm. 'And no spoilers for Season Seven of *Game of Thrones*. You know I haven't seen it yet.'

Andy humphed. 'I'll do my best.' She set about trying to make sense of the various panels, ripping open a pack of paper handkerchiefs to wipe blood from the work surfaces.

'Is there anything I can do to help?' Olivia asked before answering, 'of course there isn't. My ship doesn't have anything like this.'

'I doubt if there is anything any of us can do to help,' Erimem said. She gave Olivia a comforting pat on the arm, which Andy appreciated enormously. Olivia was completely out of her depth with technology, learning as much as she could as fast as she could, but her base knowledge was still three hundred years out of date. It was decent of Erimem to let Olivia know they were all in the same boat.

'I think I've managed to dredge up some power from an emergency reserve,' Andy said. 'Either that or we're all going to get blown to buggery.'

'I would prefer power to buggery,' Erimem said, then stopped abruptly, aware of six sets of eyes on her. 'I should rephrase that, shouldn't I?'

'Probably,' Helena said. 'Either that or get it printed on a t-shirt.'

Erimem sighed and pushed her gaffe to the back of her mind. 'How long will it take the power to build, Andy?'

Andy's lips pursed and she thought for a moment. 'Taking all the info available into consideration, I'd have to say... buggered if I know.'

That answer did not impress Erimem. 'Estimate.'

Andy sniffed. 'Five minutes maybe?'

That seemed to suit Erimem better. 'Very well. We should use those minutes to find out more about this part of the ship and look for survivors. Helena and Ibrahim, you look to the left, but be back here in five minutes. This is just getting to know where we are. Tom and Olivia, stay with Andy.' She turned to the last member of their party. 'Adam, you come with me.'

She left the room without waiting for a reply.

Helena gave Adam a sympathetic half-smile as he walked past. 'Yes, she is always this bossy when she has her Pharaoh head on.'

Adam looked even more bemused as he hurried after Erimem.

Andy watched Adam leave. 'I'd pay good money to hear that conversation.'

'Would you?' Helena shook her head. 'I wouldn't. Those are two strong personalities and they're both going to be on the defensive. It's going to be messy.'

Ibrahim nodded. 'We might not see it but there's a good chance we're going to hear it.'

'So, care to tell about all this?'

Adam had caught up with Erimem at the door of what looked like some kind of study or office.

She didn't look back at him. 'No.'

'No?' Adam repeated. 'What the hell do you mean by just saying "no" just like that?' His accent had grown broader. He sounded angry and hurt but Erimem was in no mood to compromise.

'I mean that no, I will not tell you everything about this just now,' she answered. 'Now is not the time for that discussion.'

She moved into the study and looked around. It had belonged to someone who had liked the history of sailing and cruise ships. There was a model of a liner with four smoke stacks, paintings of others on the walls and printed books which would be long out of fashion in this era in a cabinet against a wall. There were claw marks running along the spines of a dozen leather-bound books and a spray of blood across a painting of the *RMS Titanic*. Erimem placed her hand next to the books, gauging the size of the hand which had done the damage against her own hand. It was at least twice, probably closer to three times, the size of her hand.

'It took great strength to gouge the paper this way,' she murmured. 'The claws went deep.'

'Claws?' Adam asked.

Erimem frowned irritably. 'You don't think fingers could do that, do you?'

'I don't think I can be on a spaceship,' Adam snapped back.

His reply only increased Erimem's irritation. 'Given that you are obviously on a spaceship, you can tell me what you think of these marks.'

Adam bit off an angry reply. If she wanted an answer he'd damn well give her an answer. 'Considerably larger than an average man's. An average man wouldn't have the strength to slash this deep into paper.'

'I already said that.'

Adam ignored the snark. 'It's tall,' he said. 'It's bloody tall. The angle of the gouges points downwards. It must be seven feet tall. Maybe eight.'

'And the fingers?' Erimem pressed.

There was something in the angles of the fingers that was just wrong. 'Which one's the thumb?'

Erimem tapped the outer two gouge marks. 'These two.'

'Two thumbs? That's...' Adam bit off the word "impossible".
'Never mind.'

Erimem flipped through an old paper ledger on the desk.
'This is the Captain's Ready Room,' she said. 'There is nothing
about an attack in it.'

'So he didn't have time to write anything?' Adam suggested.

'The attack came quickly,' Erimem agreed. She glanced at
the writing on the page and then at the pictures in frames on the
desk – old fashioned printed pictures in actual frames rather than
a digital display. 'I would have liked this man,' she said quietly.
'He liked tradition, he loved his family, he cared for those who
served under him. He was a good leader.' She rose from the desk
and headed back out into the corridor.

Adam glanced at the photographs of the kindly middle aged
man with children he obviously adored. It was something he had
experienced before, and it always affected him. As a police
officer he had more often than he cared to remember, had to visit
a house and break the news that a loved one was dead. As often
as not, there were photographs of the dead person in the living
rooms where he usually broke people's hearts. It always felt odd,
as if they were watching him hurt the families.

'You're too soft to be a copper, Docherty.' That was what his
first sergeant had told him. Any hint that this was a show of
concern had disappeared when Sergeant Harvey had followed it
up with 'Piss off back to Jock-land where you belong.'

Like most Scots, Adam despised being called "Jock". He'd
found his revenge after his move to the detectives by being in on
the operation that arrested Sergeant Harvey for being on the take
and tipping off local villains about police raids. Odd that he
should think of Harvey now.

It didn't change the fact that he had never got over seeing
photographs of the deceased.

The next two doors yielded nothing of interest other than
more scratches and blood. They returned to the flight deck at a
run after Olivia called to them. Helena and Ibrahim arrived a few
steps behind them.

'What is it?' Erimem asked.

There were lights on some of the control panels showing that
Andy had coaxed some life back into the ship.

'Good news, bad news,' Andy said. 'The good news is...' she pressed a button and the lights came up. '...I've got the juice flowing to parts of the ship for more than just emergencies. Feel free to call me Scotty and a miracle worker.'

'And the bad news?' Helena asked.

The ship shook and a hollows *THUNK* echoed through the corridors.

'That's the bad news,' Andy said. 'We've got company.'

Erimem moved to her side. 'Can you see who it is?'

Helena indicated for the group to muster together. 'If it's the lot who did this we should just get out of here. Back to your place and then try again.'

The public address saved Andy from answering. 'This is Commander Lee of the Earth Cruiser *Saint-Saens* to any survivors on the *Andromedan Princess*. We have docked and are coming aboard.'

Erimem gave a curt nod. 'We should leave. It will do no-one any good if we have to answer their questions.'

Adam gave her a dark look. 'Somebody else whose questions you don't want to answer?'

Ibrahim's answer was on the sharp end of brusque. 'Not now, Adam.'

Helena nodded her agreement. 'Is everybody ready?'

'We've got a problem,' Andy said. 'Erimem's not in the room.'

'She's standing right there,' Adam protested.

Helena moved closer to Erimem and took a look into her glassy, lifeless eyes. 'Her body's here but her mind's somewhere else?'

Andy raised a hand to stop Adam from asking the countless questions he obviously had. 'That's something else we need to explain to you.' She peered at her friend. 'Erimem's having an ethereal chat with her grandad.'

It was an odd thing, but Erimem wasn't surprised that she was no longer on a stricken space liner but was instead sitting in a deckchair on a beach looking out into what was undoubtedly the Mediterranean. As expected, an old man with long but thinning swept-back white and a beak of a nose was sitting in the next chair. Incongruously for a Pharaoh dating from 1500BC, he was wearing a natty pair of Ray Banns and has sun cream smeared across his nose.

'Why am I not surprised to see you?' Erimem asked casually. 'I wondered if it was you who drew us off course to that spaceship?'

'Would I do a thing like that?' her grandfather asked innocently. 'How could a poor, frail old man like me do something like that? There weren't even any spaceships in my day.'

'We did not know about space in our day,' Erimem answered, 'but you and I are both very different people than we were back then.' Two glasses of fruit juice and crushed ice had appeared on a table between the chairs. Erimem sipped at one. 'Very nice.'

'Orange, passion fruit and pineapple,' her grandfather agreed. 'Your favourite.'

Erimem's nose wrinkled. 'Summer fruit cider is my favourite.'

'Yes, but I need you sober,' her grandfather chuckled. 'You have a great deal to do on that ship.'

'Do I?'

'You all do.' The old man sighed and reached for his own drink. 'Time is a complex beast,' he said slowly. 'Sometimes that is through nature and sometimes it is manipulated by those who don't understand it.'

'I know all of this,' Erimem nodded.

'But you don't know how important it is that you stay on this ship,' the old Pharaoh said. 'The future – and the past – depend on it.'

'And I will guess that you will not tell me more about it than that,' Erimem said in a resigned voice. 'If I ask for more details you give answers that are not answers and counter with riddles and...' she sought the word, '...obfuscations.'

'That is a very good choice of word,' her grandfather complimented.

'Thank you. I thought so. You will not tell me more, will you?'

The old man shook his head and his sunglasses slid a little

down his nose. He pushed them back into place. 'No. I will not.'

Erimem had expected the answer but it still irritated her all the same. 'Then will you tell me why I met Adam's grandparents on a ship the last time we travelled?'

He sniffed. 'Well, other things need kept on track as well.'

'Meaning?'

Her grandfather took a long draw on his drink. 'Meaning it's time for you to go back to your friends and let me relax in peace.

'You are very annoying, old man,' she scowled.

He simply smiled. 'I love you, too.'

With that he was gone and she was back on the flight deck of the *Andromedan Princess* surrounded by inquisitive faces.

'Well?' Andy asked. 'What did space grandad say?'

Erimem sighed. 'We are staying.'

CHAPTER FIVE

First Officer Rebecca Lee stood at the airlock of the *Saint-Saens* watching a subordinate operating the controls. While most airlocks in the galaxy were compatible, the fact that the *Adromedan Princess* had been damaged meant that protocol demanded that they play it safe. That meant deploying an inflatable docking tube between the ships in case one of the airlocks was damaged. The tube would attach itself around the outer edges of the airlocks, forming molecular bonds to the two ships and would only allow the hatches to open if the seal was airtight. Lee understood the controls better than her inexperienced crewmate. That was hardly a surprise. Her brain was infinitely superior to any of the others on board. There was no boast in that statement. It was simply the truth. She had to let others learn, though.

The light by the airlock changed from red to green and Lee gave the order for the crewman to open the hatch.

'Airlock open,' Lee reported to Captain Watson, who stood nearby at the head of what looked like the full complement of Marine Corps troops stationed on the *Saint-Saens*.

'Good,' Watson nodded. 'And the liner's airlock?'

A metal creaking and clanking answered the captain.

'Open,' Lee replied without bothering to check with the crewman at the airlock. Nothing else could have made that noise.

'Okay,' Watson nodded, 'Let's get over there.'

Lee turned to the Marines. 'Secure the immediate area on board the *Andromedan Princess*. Move in groups of three.'

The troops obeyed quickly, hurrying through the docking

tube through to the liner. Lee and Watson followed behind the troops.

Watson shivered. 'It's freezing.'

'This area was opened to space before the emergency shields came online,' Lee explained. She waved a small platoon of technicians through onto the liner. 'Cutler, take a crew down to engineering. Try to restore power to environmental systems. Get the heating system working. Meantime, Fumika – set up the temporary lighting.'

Watson gave an appreciative nod. 'Good thinking. I don't like the idea of wandering around this ship in the dark.'

'I would like to know why we detected a build-up of power from the flight deck,' Lee said thoughtfully. 'It could be automated repair systems but I want to know that for certain.'

Watson agreed quickly. 'So would I. We'll head up there. You'd better send for Captain Lescal, Lee.'

'I'm already here, captain.' A woman's clipped, precise voice caused both Watson and Lee to turns. Tall and athletic, she had short cropped dark hair, intelligent eyes and a resting face which veered towards a rather sarcastic sneer. She wore the uniform of a captain in one of Earth's oldest regiments.

'Good,' Watson said. 'We'll make for the flight deck. See what the computer records have.'

Captain Lescal moved away in a different direction than the one ordered by Watson. 'You do that, Captain Watson, I'm heading down to the living quarters.'

Lee interjected, as much to save her captain's authority as to protect Lescal. 'We haven't secured those decks yet.'

Lescal drew a powerful-looking sidearm. 'I'm armed. I can look after myself.'

Watson sighed in exasperation. Listen, aptain...'

Lescal brusquely cut across Watson. 'Captain, I'm sure I don't need to remind you that I'm army, not space-fleet, and therefore not under your command. Thanks for the ride, but I don't take orders from you.'

Watson put a hand on Lee's arm to stop the First Officer from reacting to Lescal's insolence. Lee and Lescal had clashed almost constantly during the journey, with the bulk of the confrontation being instigated by Lescal. 'Fine,' Watson said.

'Suit yourself. But I suggest that you report in every five minutes. The leaks from the engines here left our scanners unreliable at best. There's no way of knowing what's on this ship.'

'Very well,' Lescal conceded with no attempt to hide her irritation. She stalked off along the corridor.

Watson watched her go for a moment before leading Lee in the opposite direction. 'Is it just me or is that the rudest woman in the history of ever?' he asked.

'Quite possibly,' Lee answered, 'but we should remember that her sister and nephew were on board when the ship was attacked. I imagine that most humans would react in a similar manner in the circumstances.'

A pang of guilt bit at Watson's conscience. It was rather off-putting that Lee of all people should have to remind him to show a bit of human kindness and thought in the situation. 'You're probably right. Let's see what the bridge computers have to say.'

Lee pointed at a broad, plush stairway ahead. 'This way.'

'I think the power is coming up,' Andy said. 'Either that or I just set the whole ship to self-destruct.'

'What?' Tom squeaked.

'She is joking,' Erimem said.

Helena peered at Andy. 'You *are* joking, aren't you?'

'Probably,' Andy answered. 'Sort of seventy-thirty.'

'God almighty,' Adam exclaimed. 'Do you people take any of this seriously?'

'Yes,' Erimem answered.

'No,' Andy said at roughly the same time.

'A bit?' Ibrahim offered.

Helena summed up the answers. 'We take the responsibility of time travel seriously but we don't necessarily go about it in a serious way.'

'Did you just riff on Eric Morecambe to explain how we time travel?' Andy frowned.

Helena grimaced. 'More or less.'

Andy's hands moved across the controls triumphantly. 'I've got cameras up.'

'Is there a big screen we can see them on?' Erimem asked.

Andy's lips pursed. 'I think so.' She tried a few more controls and a large monitor crackled reluctantly into life. 'This was the last camera they had up.' The picture slowly cleared to show a gaping hole in a bulkhead opening the corridor directly into space.

'I'm glad we didn't arrive there,' Ibrahim muttered.

Andy inspected the readouts and tried to make sense of the display. 'There's an emergency force-field in place now so it's safe enough...' she paused uncertainly, '...so it says here anyway.'

'What about the spaceship that docked?' Erimem pressed. 'Can you find that? I would like to know who is aboard this ship.'

That sounded like a plan to Andy. She rotated through a series of cameras. The screen moved from corridor to corridor, all showing damage or blood stains until it one finally showed life. A group of six heavily armed military personnel were moving in formation along a deck, looking in each doorway. One would open the door and two would quickly enter the room and assess it for and threats. They moved with remarkable speed and efficiency, needing only seconds to find a room clear and move on. Working in two teams they took alternate doors and made swift progress along the corridor.

Erimem watched the soldiers move appreciatively. 'They are well trained.

'And they have guns,' Tom said nervously. 'A lot of guns.'

'Don't worry,' Helena said comfortingly. 'This ship came under attack. I imagine this is the rescue party.'

'Aren't they going to be a bit surprised to find us?' Tom asked. 'We're the only people on board.'

'I wouldn't say that,' Ibrahim said. He sounded as if he was trying not to be sick.'

'Jesus,' Andy breathed.

On screen the troops were standing outside a doorway. Two had removed their helmets and were vomiting.

Andy brought the interior of the room just investigated by the troops into focus.

Suddenly everyone on the flight deck looked as if they were going to be sick as well.

* * *

First Officer Lee had taken the lead in the trek to the flight deck. Even if she wearied like her colleagues she was a good deal younger that Captain Watson, though the captain did work hard to keep up. They were being tailed by troops and technical staff. The captain would never let himself look weak in front of his subordinates. They had left the plush levels of the ship behind and were now walking on the functional, beam-clean polyede flooring so beloved of both Lescal and military ships.

'Is the bridge is on this level, Lee?' Watson asked.

Lee nodded, checking the compu-pad in her hand. 'Less than twenty metres this way, captain. I can see the door-hatch ahead. It's open.'

Watson squinted in the half light. Only half of the lights were working in the corridor, presumably the ship was running in in night-mode. 'I envy your augmented vision, Lee. I can barely see the nose in front of my face.' On cue the lights flickered and then became brighter. 'They've got the power on again. That was quick.'

'Cutler's one of the best engineers in the fleet,' Lee replied. 'That's why you politicked so hard to get her transferred to the *Saint-Saens*.'

Watson showed no shame at being caught out. 'Politicked? I bribed two admirals and damn near blackmailed a third. I know at least three independent outfits who'd give their right arms to get Cutler away from the fleet. I'd have blackmailed all three if I had to.' A solitary doorway on the walls was open and shone with light. 'This way?'

Lee extended an arm across her captain's chest, barring his way. 'Wait sir.' She nodded for two troopers to go ahead. 'Netter. Flynn. Flank the door.' The soldiers did as she instructed taking positions on either side of the open door. Lee manoeuvred the captain closer to the safety of the wall. 'To the side please, Captain.'

Watson shook his head in exasperation. 'Really, Lee?'

The First Officer was unrepentant. 'Just in case, Captain.'

'Oh, very well,' Watson snorted, allowing Lee to stand ahead of him, using herself as a barrier against any danger.

Lee waved the troops forward. 'Go.'

The two troopers spun around the side of the sides of the doorway and disappeared inside. Four more troopers followed them quickly.

'Safe!' one of the troops yelled.

With Lee at his shoulder, Watson entered the bridge and was surprised to find and unlikely assortment of seven civilians standing with their hands in the air in a show of surrender.

'Oh, put your hands down,' Watson sighed. 'You all look ridiculous.'

'We are on holiday,' the smallest of the girls said. 'It is part of the tradition to look ridiculous on holiday.'

'True fact,' agreed the young woman with the red flash in her hair, who was standing at the computer controls.

'Hands down,' Watson repeated. This time the seven lowered their arms.

'Are you survivors of the attack?' Lee asked. 'Did you see who attacked your ship?'

'It is not our ship,' the small woman said. 'We arrived here after the attack.'

'How did you get here?' Lee demanded. 'Do you have a ship?'

'No...' the small woman spoke again, but her friend interrupted.

'At least not any more. Wonky connection the airlock. You didn't happen to spot a little flyer did you?' Andy asked innocently. 'Purple with red markings. We didn't get a proper seal on the airlock and it broke free.'

Watson didn't look entirely satisfied but seemed to take the explanation at face value. 'Very well. Have you found any survivors?'

The oldest of the women, she seemed to be in her early thirties, answered. 'No, we just came here to the flight deck to find out what happened, Captain...?'

'Watson,' the captain supplied, 'and this is my First Officer, Commander Lee.'

'Helena,' the older woman introduced herself before running around her group. 'My husband Ibrahim, our cousin Erimem, and our friends, Andy, Olivia, Adam and Tom.'

Watson gave each of the four a curt greeting.

'We *have* found something,' Erimem said. 'So have your men. They will be reporting soon. We watched them find it on the screen. I warn you, it is not pleasant.'

Watson squinted at the screen, picking out shapes and hues through the snowy crackling distortion. His stomach lurched. 'Are those...?'

'Bodies?' Erimem finished the question. 'Yes, they are.'

'Bits of them anyway,' Helena added. She sounded disgusted. 'They look dismembered but it's hard to tell from here. I'll know better once I've seen them.'

'Will you now?' Watson asked. 'And why would you do that?'

'Because she is a doctor,' Erimem answered sharply.

Helena nodded. 'And from your uniform, captain, I'm guessing you're not.'

Olivia spoke for the first time since the soldiers had arrived. She was hesitant but forced the words out. 'Besides, from my knowledge, abandoned ships become the claim of the first party to board them.'

Watson had no idea if that was true and looked to Lee for guidance.

The First officer nodded. 'It is an arcane law, Captain, but it remains a legal precedent.'

'Of course, we will not press our claim to this ship,' Erimem said quickly.

That didn't please Olivia. 'We won't?'

'Quiet, pirate,' hissed Andy.

'No,' Erimem said firmly, 'we will not – on the condition that we continue with our mission to help whoever is left aboard.'

'Your mission?' Lee asked. She made no attempt to hide her suspicion of these strangers. 'That sounds odd for a group of holidaymakers.'

'When we found a ship in distress it became a mission,' Erimem answered. She was equally open in her suspicion of Lee.

'Erimem was a soldier,' Helena explained to calm the waters. 'She automatically slips back into that mode when there's a crisis.'

Erimem pointed a finger at the screen. 'And I would describe those bodies as a crisis.'

Watson hid a wince as he looked back at the screen. 'Yes, I can't disagree with you on that. Which deck is that?'

Andy checked and gave the answer quickly. 'We haven't seen many other decks. We only got the juice back into the camera a bit before you arrived.'

Watson's lips pursed in thought. 'Lee, I'm going down there to see what happened. You stay here and oversee getting the ship working.' He waved towards Andy. 'And you start checking the other decks.'

'Aye-aye, cap'n,' Andy said with a hint of sarcasm. 'I must have slept through the bit where I joined up but never mind.'

Lee protested at her captain's intentions. 'Captain, I think it wiser of you remain on the bridge and...'

'I'm sure you do, Lee,' Watson interrupted, 'but I need to see this for myself. I'll be fine. I'll take a six man detail with me.'

'As you wish,' Lee conceded reluctantly.

'Doctor,' Watson said to Helena, 'will you accompany me, please? I'll be interested in hearing your opinion.'

'Of course,' Helena agreed.

Erimem moved to Helena's side. 'I will come as well. I would see what our enemy has done.' She glanced at the rest of her party. 'Stay and be as helpful as possible.'

'I'd rather see what happened down there,' Adam said, though his words were aimed at Watson rather than Erimem. 'I'm a police officer. I might be useful.'

Watson nodded his assent. 'Very well. Any of the rest of your party got useful skills?' he asked Erimem.

'All of them,' she answered quickly, 'but not, perhaps, pertinent to this situation.'

That was enough for Watson. 'All right. The rest of you stay here. Lee, get me as much information as you can.'

'Yes, captain.'

Watson indicated for six men to follow him and he headed out into the corridor with Erimem, Helena and Adam close behind.

Lee immediately set her crew to work. 'Get as many systems back on line as you can, and find the leaks that impaired the scanners.' She turned her attention to Andy. 'Now, let me see more of the ship.'

The damned woman sounded like she expected a salute in reply, Andy thought mutinously, but she simply scowled and started rotating through the cameras. Olivia had noticed Andy's irritation and tried to hide an amused smirk. Andy settled for sticking her tongue out.

Captain Cordelia Lescal moved with a confident mixture of stealth and speed through the corridors of the *Andromedan Princess*. Before leaving port she had accessed the relevant files on the liner's passenger manifest and knew which deck and cabin was her target.

She knew that she was behaving irrationally by striking off on her own without an escort, but she didn't care. She was armed and she was trained. If anything got in her way, she would blast it to atoms.

Lescal had no idea what to expect on the ship, but after taking a few sets of stairs and moving along two corridors she feared the worst. Blood and was smeared across walls and drenched the carpets. There were vile smudges of what looked like entrails on the various surfaces too. Her foot squelched in the bloody carpets as she moved. Twice she passed what looked like an attempt at a drawing in daubed blood on the bulkhead. In most situations she would have stopped and inspected them carefully. Most situations, but not this one.

The lights flickered from emergency red up to half-power night-time lighting as this deck caught up with the decks she had already passed through. Up ahead, she saw the discrete number plaque she had been searching for beside a closed door.

Closed.

That was something.

There was no blood on the door and no sign of a struggle in the immediate area either. That wasn't much bur Lescal took whatever solace she could from it.

The doors were locked and refused to respond to her touch on the pressure pad to the side of the door. She had expected that and had brought along a little bit of experimental tech being developed for military and police use. A small, black, rectangular block about the size of a personal communicator, it fit easily into her pocket but would release any legally coded door in Earth Federation space. More importantly, it would open most illegally coded doors as well, and most electronic locks used by both allied and enemy powers. Of course, that went against countless accords and treaties Earth had signed, but nobody would have expected anything else. Everyone broke their agreements with dirty tricks. Lescal didn't care how many laws of treaties she was breaching. All that mattered was getting into the suite.

The doors slid reluctantly open. Sidearm raised, Lescal went inside.

'Hello?'

There was no reply. The room was empty. She made a swift circuit of the suite. Suitcases were left open, drinks partially drunk and food half-eaten. The place had the look of having been abandoned suddenly. Baby clothes were scattered across one of the beds and a mobile communicator was carelessly tossed nearby. She picked up the small device and swiped her thumb across its ID pad. For a moment it did nothing and then slowly came to life as it accepted a close enough DNA match. She scrolled through the personal messages, wincing at the intimacy of a few and recognising a few others which she had sent herself. A folder of old school images and holographs tied a sickening knot in her stomach. All through the journey here she had avoided looking at photographs or holograms. She didn't want to think about why she was heading out to this lost ship. She didn't want to imagine what she might have found. There had been almost no signal of difficulty from the *Andromedan Princess*. Communications had simply blacked out after a single word had come through. 'Emergency!' That had been enough to send her on this very personal mission.

Lescal conducted another sweep of the suite, but found no clue as to the location of the inhabitants. Back by the bed she found herself staring at a pale yellow t-shirt with OF COURSE I'M NOISY, I'M A BABY on the front. That almost broke her. She had bought that shirt less than a fortnight earlier.

A confusing mixture of emotions hit her hard. She was relieved that she hadn't found any side of Portia and Alexander but frustrated that she hadn't found them alive, and terrified of how she might find them after the amount of blood she had seen on her way to the cabin.

But she would achieve nothing by staying in that room.

Lescal slid Portia's communicator into her pocket and started towards the door then stopped abruptly. Turning back, she scooped the yellow t-shirt from the bed and put that in her pocket too.

In the corridor, Lescal closed the door and relocked it. She didn't want just anybody tramping through the place, looking through her family's possessions.

Instinct demanded that Lescal simply search the ship from top to bottom herself, but she had to be smarter than that. She would achieve more by being part of Captain Watson's efforts.

Or at least by making use of whatever he found out.

She started back along the corridor, retracing her steps towards the flight deck.

She stopped.

There was something else in the corridor.

She could hear the stealthy movements, from just far enough around the curve in the corridor to know that whoever or whatever was there was staying just out of sight.

The hairs on the back of Commander Cordelia Lescal's neck rose. She was definitely not alone.

CHAPTER SIX

Captain Watson's party had reached the room containing the corpses within a few minutes.

'Sorry, sir,' a platoon sergeant apologised. 'A couple of the lads reacted badly to what's in there. Lost it a bit and threw up. Can't say I blame them to be honest.'

Watson moved past the sergeant into the room. It had been a small public lounge. Now it was filled with the dismembered remains of dozens, perhaps hundreds of bodies. Arms, legs, torsos and even heads were discarded haphazardly in a huge pile. The Captain suddenly looked very ill as well.

'Jesus Christ,' Adam breathed, fighting the urge to retch both at the sight in front of him but also at the stench of blood and other human matter. Blood seeped up from the carpet with every step taken towards the bodies. 'They've been cut apart.'

'No,' Erimem contradicted, 'not cut apart. Torn apart.' She pointed first at an arm and then at the lower portion of a leg. 'The cuts are not clean. The flesh is uneven and rough.'

'She's right,' Helena confirmed. The bones back it up. They're splintered rather than sliced.'

'Were they alive when this happened?' Erimem asked.

Helena thought hard for a moment. 'It's hard to be sure, but if I hard to give an answer, the blood loss would make me say yes.' She glanced up at her friend. 'What are you thinking?'

Erimem pointed at the vicious deep gouges in a chest and what looked alarmingly like bite marks on a leg. 'I recognise these,' she said quietly enough that only Helena would hear.

Helena had a dozen questions to ask but it was Adam who

asked a question first. He was staring at a symbol daubed onto the wall in blood. 'What the hell is this?'

Captain Watson had joined Adam. 'It looks like a cross of some kind,' she said. 'My men are reporting it all over the ship.'

There was some truth in Watson's assessment of the symbol being vaguely similar to a cross but Helena was not convinced. Her fingers traced the air in front of the horizontal and vertical lines. 'The positioning of these is more like a plus sign,' she said. Her fingers indicated smaller, thinner lines radiating from the point where the major lines met. These smaller lines sprayed out diagonally all around the crossing point. 'And these make it look more...'

'Like a star,' Erimem finished for her. 'It is very similar to how many pictographic languages depict a sun or a star.'

Helena nodded. 'Somebody has been paying attention in class,' she murmured absently.

'If this is all over the ship it is clearly important to the...' she caught herself. 'To the attackers. It is a rallying cry or a symbol of worship.'

'For who?' Adam demanded. 'Do you know?'

Erimem was spared from answering by the sergeant who ran in from outside. He had a finger to the comms unit in his helmet. 'It's Captain Lescal, sir. She's two levels down and says she being followed by... she said "something", sir.'

Erimem was already on her way to the door. 'Wait!' Watson shouted, but she was already out in the corridor.

'You're wasting your time,' Helena said. 'We'd better get after her.'

The party sprinted down through the corridors and stairs. Watson had no trouble in keeping up with the rest. 'That way,' he called when they had descended two decks. He pointed along the corridor. 'She was along that way.'

The ship was a kilometre and a half in length and this corridor ran at least half that distance. They heard the footsteps approaching before Captain Lescal came into view. She was sprinting, and at her heels was what looked like the devil itself. It was a little taller than a man with thin limbs covered in skin that looked wet and leathery. Its face was the face of the devil... dark, sunken eyes, a bony ridge where its nose should have been.

Human flesh hung from the needle-sharp teeth in the tops and bottom of its extended, protruding snout.

'Shoot it!' Erimem shouted at Watson's troops, 'and it moves fast so get close.'

Lescal was only half a dozen paces ahead of the creature. She was fast but her pursuer was faster.

'Get down!' Watson yelled.

Lescal threw herself low and to the side. Fire from the marines sprayed along the corridor. The creature moved with extraordinary speed and agility, leaping aside and twisting to avoid energy bolts which had seemed certain to rip into its flesh. But the creature wasn't just avoiding the blasts, it had abandoned its interest in Lescal and was still advancing on the troops. Erimem moved to the side and pulled Helena with her. Helena assumed it was to stay out of the line of fire. A moment later, Erimem held a red and white nozzle in her hand. She pointed at a button.

'When I tell you.'

Helena understood and agreed.

Erimem took three steps along the corridor, staying close to the wall. She pointed the nozzle at the creature's feet. 'Now!'

Helena hit the button. Immediately a spray of fire retarding foam shot from the nozzle in Erimem's hand and hit the deck in front of the creature, splashing up onto its feet and legs. Its feet slipped on n the foam and it lost its agility. A shot slammed into its shoulder and them another into its leg. A third hit the chest and dropped it to the deck.

'Cease fire!' Watson yelled. 'We need to interrogate it.'

'Be careful,' Erimem warned. 'It will still be dangerous.'

The troops swarmed the creature binding its arms and legs and putting a tight muzzle over its snout.

Watson crossed to where Erimem was replacing the fire hose. 'Quick thinking,' he said.

'Thank you.'

'Now tell me what that thing is,' Watson went on. 'You knew how it would move.'

Erimem nodded. 'I have seen its kind before. It is a Drofen.'

Something akin to disappointment appeared on Watson's face. 'You're wrong. The Drofen went extinct hundreds of years ago.'

Erimem didn't back down. 'Did they? Perhaps you should tell that one.'

'They had some kind of civil war and wiped each other out,' Watson persisted.

'Andy and Tom have also seen the Drofen before,' Erimem said calmly. 'They will tell you what this is.'

'Shit.' Watson gave a long moment of thought. 'All right, it's a Drofen. Which means they attacked this ship.'

'I thought as much when I saw the wounds on the dead,' Erimem admitted.

'Dead?' Lescal had joined them. Her relief at being saved faded on hearing of the discovery of human remains. 'Have you found bodies on board? Human bodies?'

'Parts of them,' Erimem confirmed. 'The Drofen are carnivores.'

Lescal physically shook. 'Where are they?' she asked quietly.

'Two decks up,' Watson said. 'Best if you don't go there. My med techs will check DNA profiles against the files.'

'Are they on board?' Lescal asked.

Watson shook his head. 'On their way.'

'Tell them to hurry,' Lescal said. She set off along the corridor.

'That looks personal,' Adam said. 'Did she have somebody on board?'

'A sister and a nephew,' Watson confirmed.

'Shit,' Helena breathed. 'She really shouldn't be up in that room.

'She's not under my command,' Watson explained. 'She used family connections to get herself a lift on my ship but I'm not her commanding officer.' His attitude softened. 'But she certainly shouldn't be up there alone.' He called his sergeant across. 'Sergeant, get that Drofen thing into a secure holding cell here on the liner. Keep it chained and locked up. I'll get more marines aboard to sweep the ship faster.'

'Yes, sir.'

* * *

'If we close down the decks your teams have swept, one of the power units could be taken off-line for repairs.'

Andy looked at Lieutenant Commander Lee, and waited for the negative reply. The First Officer of the *Saint-Saens* had so far refused every suggestion she had made, and if this one went the same way there was a good chance Andy would suggest ramming the ship and its computers where the sun didn't shine.

'That sounds sensible to me,' Lee said after a moment's thought. 'I assume there are airtight doors on each deck?'

'Several,' Andy confirmed.

'Then once my troops report that a deck is clear, seal it and take life support down to minimum,' Lee said.

'And how am I supposed to know when they're finished with a corridor?' Andy asked grumpily. 'I'm not one of your people. I don't have access to your comms.'

'True,' Lee conceded. She waved one of her subordinates forward. 'Corporal, when the patrols are finished with a deck, seal it and close it down to minimum life support.'

The corporal obediently took the next control panel along from Andy. 'Ma'am.'

'It makes more sense to split the duties,' Lee told Andy. 'Continue rotating through the camera feeds.'

'Aye, Cap'n,' Andy muttered.

'*Commander*,' Lee corrected. 'I am a commander.'

'I am a captain,' Olivia offered helpfully.

'Really?' Lees didn't even try to sound as if she believed Olivia.

'Really,' Olivia answered.

'It's true,' Ibrahim said. He was wandering around the flight deck taking in the controls and trying to make sense of them. 'It's a smaller ship than this, but Olivia is definitely its captain and her crew definitely do as they're told.'

'They do.' Olivia offered Ibrahim a smile of thanks for the support. 'We are successful.' She sniffed and then added, 'Perhaps a little too successful for our own good.'

The concern in her words certainly caught Andy's attention. 'Oho? What's that, pirate? Trouble?'

Olivia shook her head. 'Not really. It's just that times are changing and I think I must make changes as well.'

Andy glanced away from the controls quickly. 'I think this is a talk we need to have when we can focus on it.'

Olivia nodded her agreement. 'I think you are right.'

'Please focus on your task,' Lee said coolly.

'I'm multi-tasking,' Andy said sourly, turning her eyes back to the controls. 'See? I'm doing it now. Operating controls and being pissed-off with your snooty cow attitude all at the same time. It's a gift.'

Lees' head tilted and a curious frown creased her face. 'I have never been called a "snooty cow" before,' she said. 'It is a new experience. Thank you for that.'

Andy humphed. 'What's the world coming to when you can't even insult somebody anymore?' She glanced at Olivia and mouthed the word 'later' at her. Olivia nodded. Andy's attention focused on her controls and the main screen. The image changed showing a group of soldiers surrounding a captured alien creature in a pool of what looked like foam. It was a Drofen, a creature Andy had hoped she would never see again. 'Shit,' she said.

Cordelia Lescal was standing outside the passenger lounge containing the human remains when Captain Watson's party arrived. Lescal looked every bit as horrified as everyone had expected that she would. While they had all been sickened by what they had seen, none of the rest had any fear that what was left of their sister or baby nephew might be among the grisly find.

Inside the room, a team of medics were moving, taking tissue samples from the various limbs and body parts before tagging them. The DNA results were immediate allowing different components of the same person to be placed together in body-bags. A few fresh pools of vomit on the deck nearby showed that even the medics had been affected by the sights in the room.

Watson approached Lescal. 'Have they found...'

Lescal shook her head tightly but said nothing.

Helena went to a water dispenser and poured a small cup. She took it across to Lescal. 'Take this,' she said, handing the cup to her.

Lescal took the cup and downed it as if she was taking a belt of a hard drink. Erimem brought across a second cup and handed that to Lescal. This time, she sipped at the water. 'I've never seen anything like that,' she said, barely louder than a whisper.

'Nobody should ever have to see anything like that,' Helena offered sympathetically.

'Why do that?' Lescal demanded. 'Why do that to people?'

'Because we are not people to the Drofen,' Erimem said simply. 'We are food to them, nothing more.'

'Why attack now?' Helena asked. She bobbed her head towards Watson. 'You said you thought they were extinct. Why would they break out of hiding to hit this ship now?'

Lescal's fingers twitched by her holstered weapon. 'Let's interrogate that thing we caught and make it tell us.'

'It will not talk,' Erimem said with a shake of her head. 'It is a drone. Their social structure is like an insect's. They have a leader, a Prime, and that speaks for them all. The others, the drones... they will not speak.'

'You sound like you've encountered them before,' Watson said.

Erimem nodded. 'Some years ago in a war zone,' she partially explained, choosing not to mention that she had travelled through time and found the Drofen in 1942 Stalingrad during the German siege of the city. 'The Drofen we met had rebelled against the decision to be carrion feeders. They had returned to hunting live prey.'

'And?' Lescal pressed. 'What happened?'

'We killed them all,' Erimem said simply. 'They refused to leave and promised to take more humans. We blew up their spaceship and killed all of them.'

'Good,' Lescal said coldly. 'Now we know they can be beaten.'

'But it does not answer Helena's question,' Erimem said. 'Why come out of hiding now?'

Watson puffed his cheeks out and exhaled. 'I wonder...'

'Wonder what?' Lescal demanded.

Captain Watson sucked on his lower lip. 'It's something Lieutenant Commander Lee has been observing. Stories of attacks in outer colonies. Why the Venulatu system seems to have gone dark. Better get her to do the debrief.'

The conversation was halted as a medic crossed to join them. She was smeared with blood and had an uncomfortable look on her face, as if she would rather be anywhere other than giving this report.

'What is it, Garcia?' Watson asked.

'It's for Captain Lescal,' Garcia said. 'You asked us to alert you when a DNA signature popped. We've found it.' She passed her tablet to Lescal. 'I'm sorry.'

The tablet dropped from Lescal's numb fingers.

No-one had the time to console Lescal. Lieutenant Commander Lee's voice sounded in Captain Watson and Lescal's ears. 'Captain, it's Lee. The civilians up here have identified the alien you caught as a Drofen and, Captain, there's a second one caught in a corridor just above you. Its leg is caught in one of the emergency doors. The leg looks broken.'

'Take it captive,' Watson said. 'Keep it separate from the other one.'

'Don't bother.' Lescal was on the move, running towards the stairs. 'I'll deal with it.'

'Lescal!' Watson called. 'Lescal!'

Lescal ignored the captain and kept moving.

'Damn it!' Watson spat. 'Come on. We can't let her face that thing alone.' They all ran after Lescal.

Erimem and her friends passed Watson quickly and caught up with Lescal around twenty metres from the injured Drofen. The creature was weak, possibly delirious. The Drofen's leg had stopped the door from closing fully but the opening was only five or six centimetres. It had suffered heavy blood loss when its leg had been trapped by a closing security door. The leg was compressed so much that the bone inside would have to be crushed. The skin had split and dark red, almost purple blood had poured to the floor.

The Drofen lifted its awful hands defensively but its movements were weak and vague. Its eyes struggled to focus on Lescal as she approached.

'It needs medical treatment,' Helena said, peering at the Drofen. 'Nothing's going to survive that kind of blood loss without it.'

'You're right.' Lescal drew her blaster and strode towards the

Drofen. With every step she squeezed the trigger. Blast after blast of superheated energy slammed into the Drofen. Its body glowed, its skin blistered and boiled until it turned black and flaked away leaving just the charred husk of the Drofen. It smouldered and the corridor stank of charred flesh.

Lescal holstered her weapon and took the final few steps towards the dead Drofen. She slammed the sole of her boot into the Drofen's head, crushing it.

'There was no need for that,' Watson said angrily.

Adam was crimson with fury. 'It was defenceless! It couldn't defend itself! That was murder!'

'And it was murder when these Drofen killed my sister and my nephew,' Lescal yelled back. 'We couldn't interrogate it. It was dying from blood loss. I did it a favour!'

'This will go on the record,' Watson said severely. 'It will probably cost you your commission.'

'Do you think I really care?' Lescal answered. 'Throw me in the brig if you want. I've already lost everything worthwhile.' She turned and walked away.

Several hours later Captain Watson summoned Captain Lescal to a meeting in the Briefing Room aboard the *Saint-Saens*. Lieutenant Commander Lee was also present along with half a dozen other senior officers as well as the civilians from the *Andromedan Princess*.

'You haven't wasted time calling an inquiry?' Lescal said bitterly.

'Please sit,' Captain Watson said, indicating an empty chair, 'and this isn't a courts martial. At least for now,' he added grumpily.

'Then what is it?' asked Lescal.

'If you would, Mr Lee?' Watson said, indicating for Lee to take over.

The First Officer took her cue. At her nod, a diagram showing the projected course of the *Andromedan Princess* appeared on a large monitor. 'This is the flight path of the *Andromedan Princess*.' A small image of the liner appeared on the monitor, radiating a pulsing outline. 'And this is its current location.' She nodded again and the liner's position moved further back along the projected course. 'However, this is the location at which the attack took place before the ship started to drift. It is also the location at which the ship's escape pods were launched. Some of those pods were shot down by the attacking ship but a number escaped and made planet-fall on the nearest world, Kestra. Their long range beacons were picked up before we arrived here.' Lee's focus turned to Lescal. 'We are all aware that your sister's remains were found on the *Saint-Saens*, and you have the condolences of everyone aboard.'

'Keep your mechanical sympathy,' Lescal said bitterly. 'Robots don't feel sympathy.'

'But we androids do,' Lee said, sounding so resolutely un-annoyed that there was no doubt that the insult had pained her, 'and the crew's sympathy is genuine. However, no remains of your nephew were found, and the data most recently returned by one of the landed pods is clear, that its sole passenger was a male infant of your nephew's age.'

It took a moment for Lescal to fully understand the meaning of Lee's words. 'You're saying Alexander is alive?'

'I am saying that he was alive when he landed on this planet,' Lee answered. 'We are too far out to make voice contact with the pods at this time.'

'We need to go there,' Lescal said to Watson. 'Now. We need to go there now. To Kestra.'

'We're charging engines and we'll be under way in an hour,' Watson replied. 'We need the *Andromedan Princess* with us to house the survivors. Her repairs are going through final checks but I'm informed she will keep the pace with us without any difficulty.'

'How long?' Lescal demanded. 'Till we get to Kestra? How long?'

'Thirteen hours, forty one minutes,' Lee answered.

'Thanks.' Cordelia Lescal stood and headed for the door. 'I'll be in my cabin.' She strode out into the corridor. As soon as the doors slid closed behind her, Lescal ran for her cabin. She closed the door and locked it before collapsing to the metal floor by her bed. She had gone on this mission not knowing what to expect. What she had found had been worse than anyone could ever have anticipated. Her sister had been eaten alive by those Drofen bastards. She had thought Alex had suffered the same fate and the lack of any DNA evidence was simply down to him being so tiny. But now she knew he had escaped. He had gone into an escape pod. How had he wound up in a pod alone? Portia would never have just left him there. She must have had a reason. Had she fought off one of those monsters to save her son?

For hours Cordelia Lescal had wept bitter and angry tears at the loss of her family. Now, with hope returned that at least one of them was alive, she broke down and cried uncontrollably again. This time the tears were fuelled by fear that the hope being dangled in front of her was going to be taken away. She couldn't bear the thought of losing Alex twice. The universe couldn't do that to her. It couldn't steal her hope away. Hope was all she had left, but she knew that hope could be far more brutal than despair.

Alone and behind her locked door, Cordelia Lescal lost control and wept until exhaustion took her into the mercy of sleep.

'We're sleeping on the liner,' Andy informed her party, as they headed back across the horribly wobbly docking tube onto the *Andromedan Princess*.

'Is there a reason we're not on the ship with all the guns?' Tom asked nervously.

Erimem answered. 'They do not have room for us and this ship has many rooms which were empty during the voyage. We will be in those so that we do not take rooms from those who died.'

'We're not in rooms,' Andy corrected, 'we're in suites. The empty accommodation was all in the most expensive part of the ship so we are on level *Swanko de Posh* as it is now known in my head. Olivia and I already put our luggage up there – thank us later – and I'll show you all the way.'

'Nicely done,' Ibrahim offered appreciatively. 'Have you been watching repeats of *The Love Boat*?'

Andy sucked her teeth for a moment. 'You got a problem with 1970s tat television, Mr Hadmani?' she asked accusingly.

'Of course not,' Ibrahim answered before adding quietly,

'I'm too young to remember it.'

'That's a dig at me,' Helena said with a weary smile. 'My husband is a bad man and he is not getting kissed before bed tonight.'

They all collected their cases and moved onto the Presidential Deck.

'There are eight suites,' Andy said. 'They're all the same size and I've got keys for five of them.

'Lucky dip,' Helena said, plucking a set of electronic keys from Andy's hand without checking the number. She held it up. 'Three,' she said. 'We're in three.'

Olivia plucked a set from Andy and peered at the number. 'Four.'

'We're in four,' Andy confirmed.

Erimem pushed Adam's hand away from the keys and picked a set. 'Adam and I are in two,' she announced. When Andy's eyebrows made a bolt up her forehead in surprise Erimem added. 'Shut up.'

'So I'm bunking alone?' Tom sounded on edge at the thought.

'We can shift things around,' Ibrahim offered. 'I can bunk down with you or maybe Adam can...'

Tom shook his head. 'No, it's okay, thanks. I'm just kinda out of practice at this. I'll be fine in...' he took a key from Andy. '...One. I'm in one.'

Ibrahim pointed back along the corridor. 'There's a bar along there. Once we're settled I'm raiding it for a drink. Anybody else up for that? Tom?'

The offer was clearly made to make the younger man feel more comfortable and Tom leaped at it. 'I'll be there in ten.'

'Free booze?' Andy said to Olivia.

'A pirate never turns down free grog,' Olivia agreed.

'I will also be there,' Erimem said.

'So will I, Adam added.

As the group split to go to their cabins, Erimem glanced back and caught Andy's eye. Her friend mimed kissing and pointed at Adam.

Erimem simply mouthed back a silent 'Shut up!'

* * *

The Presidential Suites aboard the *Andromedan Princess* quite easily put any hotel from the early Twenty First Century to shame. The furnishings were stylish, elegant and timeless. The reception room was at least as large as most flats and Adam commented that even just the bathroom was bigger than his whole flat. The single bedroom was around half the size of the reception room and had the plushest carpet Adam had ever sunk into.

'There is only one bed,' Erimem said quickly. 'That does not mean we are going to have sex here tonight.'

'You're fucking right it doesn't,' Adam said. They were both surprised by quite how angry he sounded.

'You have many questions to ask,' Erimem said in a cool voice that was straying towards cold after his angry reply. 'This is the best way for us to talk about your questions.'

'Questions?' Adam said. 'Questions like, oh, I don't know... let's start with "What the fuck is going on?" and go from there.'

'You know what is happening,' Erimem answered, moving into the mindset she used when talking politics at court in Thebes. Getting angry never got her anywhere there and it would do no good if she and Adam both lost their tempers here. 'We have travelled in time.'

'Bollocks.'

'Do you have another explanation for why you have been on two spaceships in the past hour?'

'Drugs?' Adam offered hopefully.

She shook her head sadly. 'We have travelled in time,' she repeated.

Adam slumped into the incredibly comfortable couch. 'But that's impossible. I saw Brian Cox on telly saying time travel was impossible. Stephen Hawking said it as well, I think.' He shrugged. 'I tried reading his book but I didn't understand it.'

Erimem sat on the couch as well, leaving a good metre between them. 'I don't understand the technical and mechanical side of time travel either. Andy is the only one who has any understanding of it.'

Adam's eyebrows shot up. 'Andy who makes the bacon rolls

understands time travel?'

'Andy, who is the most intelligent person at the university and who works in the canteen so that she can look after her brother because their parents both died,' Erimem corrected sharply, 'Andy understands some of the time travel mechanics.'

Adam took a moment to assimilate that. 'Did she build it?'

'No,' Erimem answered.

'So how did you get it?'

'That is a long story,' Erimem said.

Adam's shrug was what Andy would have called "passive aggressive" or "twat-ish" depending on her mood. 'We've got time travel,' Adam said. 'Surely that means we've got time?'

It was understandable that he would be frightened and angry. Erimem just knew that this was not going to be a good conversation. 'We appropriated it a few years ago,' she said, 'when I was brought to the Twenty First Century.'

'Where do you appro...' Adam stopped halfway through one question when another came screaming into his head. 'You were *brought* to the Twenty First Century?'

'Yes.'

'So you're not *from* the Twenty First Century? When are you from? The future? The Fortieth Century?' Adam's face froze. 'Are you an alien?'

'No,' she replied as patiently as she could manage, 'I am human and I am Egyptian,' she paused before ploughing on, 'I was born in the Royal Palace at Thebes in the Fifteenth Century FC.'

Adam visibly paled. 'Fifteenth Century? BC?'

'Yes.'

'I think my brain just exploded.'

'If you do not believe me, I can show you my death mask when we get back to London. It is in our museum's exhibit along with the artefacts taken from the tomb I shared with my brothers. It is a very good likeness of me.'

Adam rested his face in his hands. 'I bet nobody has ever said that sentence before.' His head jerked round abruptly. 'Wait a minute. That's a *Pharaoh's* death mask you have in the museum.'

Erimem nodded slowly. 'Yes. It is mine.'

'So you're a Pharaoh?'

'Yes.'

'And you travel in time?'

'Yes.'

'Christ, I need a drink.'

'You are not the only one,' Erimem muttered.

'You're a time travelling Pharaoh?' Adam repeated. 'And you choose to live in London in 2020?'

Erimem nodded defensively. 'It is where my family and friends are. Well, Olivia doesn't live in...'

'London or 2020?' Adam asked.

'2020. Or London. Either.'

He became even paler. 'She's not from 2020 either?'

'No.'

'When *is* she from?'

'More than three hundred years ago,' Erimem answered.

'Well, that's a long-distance relationship for you,' he muttered.

'They make it work,' Erimem said, unsure if he was being critical of her friends.

She could almost hear the cogs turning in Adam's brain. 'So when Andy called Olivia a pirate...'

Erimem nodded. 'She is a pirate captain, though she uses the term "privateer" for her work.'

'So there's a Pharaoh and a pirate?'

Erimem nodded again. 'Yes.'

'So, where do Ibrahim and Helena come into this?' he said, 'and I am almost afraid to ask that.'

'Ibrahim is my nephew,' Erimem answered, 'or my great-nephew man, many, many generations down the line. He is a direct descendant of my brother, Mentu.' She paused and looked at Adam with concern. 'Do you want to stop or continue?'

'Oh, let's go on,' he said, sounding more stunned and bemused by the minute. 'How much weirder can it get?'

'Helena is two and a half thousand years old and used to be immortal but she gave it up to save Ibrahim's life in Victorian Africa,' Erimem blurted. She winced when she saw Adam's face. 'That was not a serious questions about how much weirder things could get, was it?'

He just stared at her for a moment. 'No.'

'Sorry,' she grimaced.

He rubbed his hands across his eyes and leaned forward. 'That's all true? All of it?'

'Yes,' she answered. 'All of it.'

'And is there more to tell?

Erimem sank back into the couch and blew her cheeks out. 'Much more.'

'Shit.' Adam stood and headed for the door. 'I think I'm going to need that drink with Ibrahim before I hear any more.'

Erimem followed him to the door. 'You're not the only one.'

Given the nature of their experiences during the day and Adam's shell-shocked reaction to what he had stumbled into, the drinks in the lounge turned out to be a far more relaxing experience than anyone had expected. It helped that they were very expensive drinks and they were all on the house.

'So, is everybody at the university in on this time travel thing?' Adam asked.

'No, just us,' Ibrahim answered.

Andy held up a finger. 'Point of order, Mr Speaker – us and Trina.'

'True,' Ibrahim conceded. 'Us and Trina.'

'Trina?' Adam frowned. 'Geordie Trina? Spends time in the offices?'

'*Mackem* Trina,' Andy said. 'She's a Sunderland supporter, not Newcastle.'

'Time travel wasn't for her,' Helena said quietly. 'She's lovely but she got too involved.'

Adam waved a finger around the lounge. 'And we're not involved here?'

'It is complicated,' Erimem said. 'She risked damaging the future. There is responsibility in time travel.'

'And lots of fun,' Andy added.

Erimem smiled fondly at her friend. 'Yes, and lots of fun.'

Helena nodded her agreement. 'I get to visit places I haven't been in centuries and see friends I never thought I'd see again.'

Ibrahim shrugged. 'I'm shallow. I just use it to go to classic football matches. When you see Carlos Alberto score the greatest goal ever in the 1970 World Cup Final, I know exactly where I am in the crowd... twice.'

'You went to the same game twice?' Helena shook her head in utter bemusement. 'You never told me that.'

Ibrahim smiled benignly. 'And this reaction is why.' He sniffed. 'Besides, have I ever complained about how many times you three go to see Elvis?'

'That's different,' Andy protested. 'He's a mate.'

'Okay, I get all of that,' Adam said, 'especially the gigs and the football, but I'm guessing it's not all fun.'

'No,' it was Tom who answered, 'it's not.' He turned quiet as he became aware that all eyes were on him. 'Sorry, I didn't mean to bring things down.'

'You didn't' Helena said encouragingly. 'Just say what you feel.'

Erimem added her backing. 'Please go ahead.'

Tom began to speak, though it was more as if he was speaking to himself than the rest of the group. 'That first time we travelled, back to Greece, to Cleopatra's army...' Erimem held up a hand to stop Adam from interrupting and Tom continued, '...I still dream about Anna. Not dreams... nightmares.' He glanced over to Adam. 'She was a Fresher. The police asked me questions about her a few years ago.'

'I know who you mean,' Adam nodded. 'She disappeared before I was assigned here.'

'She was murdered in ancient Greece,' Tom said, his voice thick with guilt, 'and it was my fault she was there.'

'Why was it your fault?' Andy asked.

'If I hadn't picked her up the night before...'

Andy interrupted, 'She'd still have come into the café for her breakfast. She hadn't settled in yet. She was living out of the café for meals.'

Helena sighed. 'Look, you didn't make the decision to drag people through time. That wasn't your doing. It was those bastards who wanted to kill Erimem. They killed Anna, not you.'

'If anybody is responsible it's probably me,' Ibrahim said sombrely. 'I worked with them. I should have known there was something wrong about them.'

'Who are you talking about?' Adam asked. 'People you worked with? Are you saying the academics who went missing...'

'Murderous time travelling cult,' Andy nodded. 'They sacrificed a couple of kids, murdered Anna and dragged Erimem through time so they could kill her.'

'Jesus Christ,' Adam breathed. 'How the fuck do I put that in a police report?'

'None of the crimes were committed in the UK,' Andy explained, 'or in your time, and most of them not on this planet. Her mouth quirked. 'Or even in this universe if we're being pedantic.'

'Doesn't mean I don't bring them in,' Adam said. 'Where are they?'

'Dead,' Erimem said simply. 'They are all dead. They went to war with us. They did not win.'

Adam visibly stiffened. 'You killed them all?'

Erimem raised her chin defiantly. 'Yes.'

'In self-defence,' Ibrahim agreed.

Helena tugged at Ibrahim's shirt. 'Show him.'

Ibrahim sighed and opened his shirt showing a scar on the front of his torso. He turned and let Adam see the matching wound at the back. 'That's what they did to me. With swords.' The usual spark of fun dimmed briefly in Ibrahim's eyes. The memory of that attack still woke him at night. 'I'd have been dead without Helena.'

'How did you kill them?' Adam asked. He sounded very much like he was on duty, getting information about a crime.

Erimem explained, 'We stopped their demon lord from manifesting in this world. It killed most of them in its rage.'

'Demon?'

Andy nodded. 'Yep. Ancient Egyptian death cult demon.'

Adam's head dipped. 'Okay,' he said in resignation, 'I quit.'

Ibrahim poured Adam another drink. 'Here.'

'Thanks. I need it.' Adam took a healthy gulp at his dram.

'We don't go looking for fights,' Andy said.

Helena's face scrunched in a grimace. 'Usually,' she added. 'We don't *usually* go looking for fights.'

'Fair enough,' Andy agreed. '*Usually*.'

'Normally, we just try to mind our own business and help people if they need it,' Erimem said.

'I'm not really involved in this,' Tom said, 'but I have seen you do good, like the way you helped that Russian woman and her kids in Stalingrad.' His face darkened. 'That was where we saw those Drofen things.'

'You said it was a war zone,' Adam said to Erimem, and a frown creased his forehead. 'Stalingrad during the war?'

'1942,' Andy provided. 'Bloody freezing, it was.'

Adam slumped back in his seat. 'I'm going to need a bigger drink.'

Helena laughed and smiled with encouragement. 'You're doing fine. Most people go a bit loopy with the whole time travel thing.'

'I did,' Olivia agreed. 'I tried to run away but where could I run. I was in the future.' She beamed at Adam. 'Now I love it. I even like coffee now.'

Andy feigned offence. 'I thought it was *me* you came to the Twenty First Century for.'

'And also for you.' Olivia said dutifully.

Adam opened his mouth and closed it again. The words wouldn't come. He tried again. Nope. Still nothing. Finally he found his words. 'I can't get over how matter of fact you are about this.'

'Because for us it *is* fact,' Erimem said. 'It is not like everyone else's life, and it is not easy to understand. As Helena said, it is not for everyone.'

Andy supported her friend. 'So maybe you understand why we're a bit reluctant to tell people about things?'

'Who would believe you?' Adam asked. 'I'm sitting here on a spaceship in the future and I don't believe it.'

'You will get used to it,' Olivia said. 'I did. And I am just a pirate.'

'Privateer,' Andy corrected.

Olivia's hair shimmered as she shook her head. 'Pirate is sexier.'

Adam took another sip of his whiskey. 'Okay,' he said. 'Where else have you all been? Tell me where you've been, what you've done.'

Ibrahim pushed the bottle of vintage Glenmorangie 2377 across to Adam. 'You're going to need this.'

The drinks lasted for just over an hour. Seeing Adam coming to terms with this impossible new life helped Tom come out of his shell. They were nothing alike as people but the joint experience of being the outsiders of the group gave them some common ground, which helped keep Tom involved in the conversation. By the end of the night everyone had relaxed at least to some extent.

Helena took Ibrahim's arm and Andy draped an arm around Olivia's waist as they went back into their suites, saying friendly goodnights as they went. Even Tom was relatively open and relaxed.

Erimem yawned and emerged from that bathroom. She had changed into a pair of Minnie Mouse pyjamas. She found Adam in the reception room, laying a blanket out on the sofa.

'What are you doing?' she asked.

'Making up a bed?'

'Why?' she asked. 'We have a very comfortable bed through here.'

'I know,' Adam explained slowly, 'but we're no'... y'know...'

Erimem headed for the bedroom . 'I promise I will not... oh, what is the phrase Andy uses? Yes, I promise I will not jump your bones.'

'But can *you* trust *me*?' Adam asked.

'Of course,' she answered lazily. 'If you tried anything I could break you in two.' She yawned again. 'But I would rather not do that. We are friends who will share a bed because we are sharing this suite. We have a long day ahead tomorrow. You will sleep better in a bed.' She disappeared through into the bedroom. 'And turn that light out when you come through.'

Adam found a pair of complementary pyjamas and changed into them. They were made for someone considerably chunkier than he was but at least it spared him from getting into bed in his boxers and t-shirt.

Erimem had already chosen her side of the bed and was snuggled under a particularly warm looking cover. Adam slid into the bed and turned the light out, making sure he stayed securely on his side of the bed. He had spent a lot of time with this unusual, funny, fascinating Egyptian and he knew there was a spark between them. He had wondered if they would ever wind up in bed together. He had never thought it would be on a spaceship in the middle of who-knows-where on their way to some planet or other. He yawned. He was tired and the booze was going to make sleep come quickly.

'You did well today,' Erimem said quietly. 'You faced a hard day and you did well. Tomorrow will be easier.'

'You think so?'

He heard her chuckle. 'Probably not. Go to sleep.'

A few minutes later, Adam Docherty was asleep.

CHAPTER SEVEN

The inner sanctum of Vallaren's temple was older than ancient. The stone floors and steps had grooves worn in them by hundreds of years of footsteps. The walls and pillars were adorned with the most bizarre of carvings which mixed violent religious images with scientific formulae as DNA resequencing vied for surface space with a vengeful god blasting its followers into oblivion with lightning fire from its outstretched hands.

Vallaren himself knelt in front of an altar above which hovered a three dimensional image of what seemed to be a blazing star with for sharp points protruding at the four prime points of the compass to give the effect of a sort of a cross.

A heavily scented incense wafted across from one of the low burners arranged at frequent intervals around the walls. Vallaren inhaled deeply, savouring the pungent aroma. He had come to this place for so long that the smell had become part of his worship.

He heard the scraping footsteps on the stone and recognised the gait immediately. Over the years he had learned that everyone had a distinctive way of walking, whether it was a rhythm of step or a limp or a way of catching their heel and scuffing the ground with it. Footsteps were as individual as a fingerprint.

'Come in, my friend,' he said. The tallest of the Drofen entered the sanctum. Vallaren smiled at the fearsome creature. 'You are back, my brother. You were successful.'

The Drofen spoke. It was the Horde Prime, by ancestry the dominant Drofen, the most developed and intelligent of its kind, and the only one capable of speaking the human language. 'The ship was purified, Father Vallaren,' it said in reverential tones.

Vallaren looked at the Drofen Prime with a paternal affection. 'We never held any doubt that you would carry out the Almighty's commands,' he said. 'Were any survivors left on the ship?'

'None,' the Prime answered, obviously trying hard to suppress its pride.

Vallaren had already looked at the Prime's ship logs while it was en route back to homeworld, but he had to let his subordinate have its moment by giving a full report. 'And the escape pods?'

'Some escaped,' the Prime answered, 'but that was expected. We destroyed many of the pods to save the souls inside.'

Vallaren patted the Prime's arm affectionately. 'You will be blessed for your efforts,' he said. 'Did we lose any of our brothers?'

Something close to a sigh escaped from the Prime's leathery throat. 'Two souls did not return. We believe they were killed by the ship's defences.'

Vallaren bowed his head in prayer. 'The first martyrs of our Holy Crusade, but not the last.' He squeezed the Prime's arm. 'If we are fortunate, we will all join them, burning in the fire of absolution.'

He sounded as if he was desperately looking forward to the flames in his zeal.

'We must pray for them,' the Prime said, dipping its head in obeisance.

Vallaren placed a hand on the Prime's back and eased him towards the altar. 'I will join you. We shall pray for all of us.'

'It pains me that the pods escaped our guns,' Prime said sadly.

'You think you have failed the souls in those escape pods?' Vallaren asked sympathetically.

'They should have been free. Instead they have landed on a primitive world where they will suffer.'

'Do you want to go back and give them freedom?' Vallaren asked.

'Yes,' the Prime answered. 'I believe we owe it to them, to our Godhead and to our crusade.'

'Then you should go,' Vallaren said with conviction. 'What is the first thing we are told we must do?'

'We must always be true to our beliefs,' the Prime answered automatically.

'Then go,' Vallaren said fondly. 'Go and ease your conscience. Help those poor souls find their peace.'

'Thank you, my father.'

The Prime turned and retreated the way it had come.

The conversation had gone almost exactly as Vallaren had predicted that it would. The Drofen were loyal and reliable subordinate and one of their greatest qualities was quite how predictable they were. The drones followed their Prime and the Prime followed Vallaren. That meant that he had the most loyal following, each one of them dedicated to their holy cause. He had waited for so long for them to come to him. Ever since his epiphany, he had known what he had to do; he had known his followers would come. They would help him bring rapture to the universe.

Erimem woke with a feeling of warm and relaxation.

Her eyes opened sharply.

She also had the feeling of a body pressed close against her back. She turned and saw the back of a dark head on the pillow beside her. Adam hadn't decided to try his luck. They had simply moved closer in the night and wound up sleeping back to back in the middle of the bed. She had read about what sleeping positions in couples meant in a book Andy had given her on body language. According to her book, this back to back position meant that they were relaxed and comfortable together. She was pleased for what that said about Adam. He had been faced with a lot that previous day and he had come through it more or less intact, and he hadn't run for the spare suite.

Relationships were not Erimem's strong suit. At least not romantic relationships. Her friendship with Andy was something she understood and that meant she understood how Olivia fitted into her life too. Ibrahim and Helena were her family by blood, and Andy and Olivia were her family by choice. The relationships with other people at the university... she understood those too. Security Dan, the fifty-something who patrolled the campus during the day always made her smile with stories of his wife and their children – and now grandchildren. She understood her tutors, she understood, the people she worked with in her role as Ibrahim's assistant. Romance, though, that was different. It was complicated. Things were different in the Twenty First Century than they had been in her father's palace. She had known what fate had likely awaited her even if it was not something she would have enjoyed. The freedom to choose the man or woman she would give her heart to... that was something she had never anticipated. Putting down roots in one place had never been her plan either. Even after arriving in London she had always assumed that she would move on at some point. But she was still there, still at the university and still happy with her family. It was too early to know if Adam Docherty had a place in her long-term future, but for now, she was content to have him in her present.

She contemplated sliding her arm over his waist. No, that would be too intimate a thing to do. It would send him messages she did not want to send. Did she?

She would think about that later. Moving slowly so that she didn't wake Adam, Erimem slipped out of bed and made her way to the bathroom.

'Sleep well?' Andy asked Erimem.

'You mean, did we have sex?' Erimem answered.

'I was being subtle.'

Erimem snorted. 'You are *never* subtle,' she replied. 'But to answer your questions, yes, I slept very well and no, we did not have sex.'

Andy grimaced. 'You're no fun.'

'He is a gentleman,' Erimem said, 'and also, he does not snore.'

'Does he starfish in bed?'

Erimem's eyebrow's lifted. 'Is that something perverted I have never heard of?'

Andy gave her a sour look. 'It means does he...' she threw her arms out wide. 'Does he steal the whole bed?'

'Oh.' Erimem shook her head. 'No, he stayed on his side.'

'He's a keeper,' Andy said sagely. 'Olivia's a restless sleeper. The only way I can avoid getting a black eye is to grab her and cuddle her.'

'I'm sure you hate that,' Erimem sniffed.

They had been the first to return to the executive lounge, which had become the unofficial meeting place. They had cleared the previous night's glasses away and programmed the food dispenser to prepare breakfast for everyone.

The group assembled over the next half hour and ate quickly before heading up to the flight deck where a skeleton crew of Watson's officers were operating the ship. Most of the crew were junior officers and recognised them from the day before.

The junior lieutenant, who looked like he should still be in school, delivered a message to Erimem's group. 'Captain Watson asked to talk to you as soon as you were awake.'

'Where can we speak to him?' Erimem asked.

'Here is fine, ma'am,' the lieutenant answered. 'I can put it on the main viewer.'

Erimem agreed quickly. 'Do so.'

Captain Watson's appeared on the view-screen. The engineers from the *Saint-Saens* had done a good job working through the night, repairing the communications so that the picture and sound were pristine. 'Good morning,' Watson said. 'You're having an early start over there.'

'As are you,' Erimem agreed. 'I trust you have managed at least some sleep?'

Watson appeared amused at being cajoled by a member of the public. 'My First Officer insisted on it. She is... persuasive.'

'Good,' Erimem answered. She moved on, becoming all business. 'You asked to speak with us?'

'I did,' Watson confirmed. 'We'll be in orbit around Kestra in an hour or so. I'll be shuttling teams down to the surface as soon as we arrive. I've got crew split across two ships now...'

Erimem saw the captain's meaning and interrupted. 'Of course we will help in any way we can. We will be happy to join you in the shuttles.'

Watson smiled gratefully. 'That's what I thought you'd say. We appreciate it. When we make orbit we'll link up our two ships and get you across. We'll be sending four shuttles to the surface. The pods should have landed all together but they seem to be in batches. It's a jungle world so there may be a fair bit of searching involved.'

Erimem looked around her group and was met by nods from them all. 'We understand,' she told Watson. 'We will be ready when the ships join.'

'Excellent,' Watson said. 'We'll see you then.'

With an oxygen/nitrogen atmosphere, abundant water, nutrient-rich soil and a mass and therefore gravity ninety percent that of Earth, Kestra was a world which might have been ideal for human colonisation were it not for the perpetual rain, the painfully humid conditions and the extraordinarily aggressive indigenous life. It was a planet Earth would at some point turn its eyes to, but as yet, Kestra was just too much trouble to have been given serious consideration for colonisation. *Yet.*

The North and South Poles of Kestra were gleaming white ice caps, considerably larger than those on Earth. The three major continents were almost entirely covered with forests, though the central band of the planet was more accurately described as tropical jungle.

The escape pods had landed in four general areas on two of the continents. They should have landed in one concentrated grouping but Lees hypothesised that feedback through the ship's systems caused by the attack had caused a minor malfunction in the guidance computers.

Erimem's group had been split between three of the shuttles. Erimem, along with Helena and Adam, were assigned to the shuttle landing on the east coast of the imaginatively named Continent Two along with Lieutenant Commander Lee and Captain Lescal. The signal from the escape pod which had contained Lescal's nephew came from that area.

Andy, Olivia and Tom were assigned to the southern tip of Continent Two, which seemed to be engulfed by a blizzard stretching up from the South Pole, while Ibrahim had volunteered to join the party sent to the northern tropical jungles of Continent Two.

The shuttles themselves were ugly, bulky grey ships which operated by brute force rather than aerodynamics. In space they handled well enough but inside the atmosphere the shuttles shook and vibrated violently.

On their ship, Erimem and Helena gritted their teeth and waited for the turbulence to stop. Adam, on the other hand, looked like he was ready to vomit all over his borrowed uniform.

'It will be over soon,' Erimem told him through gritted teeth.

Adam just screwed his eyes shut all the tighter.

Finally, after an eternity, the shuttle made a stiff, bumpy landing. The hatch hissed open and they all gratefully stepped out into a clearing in the forest. Around ten metres away, what could only have been an escape pod was partially embedded in the ground. Another five metres further on was a second escape pod, though it appeared to have had a softer landing. I large bonfire blazed between the two pods. Half a dozen faces peered from fhat farthest of the pods. Their expressions changed from fear and apprehension to relief at the sight of their rescuers.

Lescal pushed past the rest of her party and ran towards the survivors. 'Is there a baby here?' she demanded. 'Where's my nephew? Where's Alex?'

Confused and blank expressions looked back at her. 'I'm sorry,' a young man in the tattered uniform of a steward answered, 'we didn't have a baby aboard either of our pods.'

'You must have!' Lescal snapped.

'There are two more pods within ten kilometres of here,' Lees said calmly. 'Your nephew must be in one of those, Captain Lescal.'

Lescal turned an angry gaze on the survivors. 'Why haven't you tried to get to the other pods? You must know they're near here.'

'We saw them land,' the steward agreed, 'but there was no way we could get through that forest.'

'Why not?' Lescal demanded. 'It's only ten kilometres.'

'Ten kilometres through a jungle full of predators,' the steward answered.

'There are animals in there,' a haggard woman added. She sounded shrill and brittle. They took my husband the first few minutes we were here.' She shivered violently. 'I still hear him screaming.'

'It's why we have the fire blazing,' the steward said. 'They don't like it, and it just about keeps them out of the clearing.'

Erimem had been listening to the conversation. 'Can the shuttle find the other pods and take us to them?'

'Yes,' Lee answered, 'but there is no other clearing for thirty kilometres. The shuttle will not be able to land.'

'Then we must find another way to reach them,' Erimem said, 'and I do not think going directly through the forest is an option.'

'Do you have something in mind?' Lescal demanded, 'or do you just like the sound of your own voice? You're a damn civilian anyway. I don't need to listen to you.'

'But you do need to listen to me,' Lee interrupted coolly, 'and Captain Watson has suggested I make use of Miss Erimem's experience when appropriate.'

'God,' Lescal spat, 'so I'm stuck listening to a civilian and a toaster. Great.'

'What the hell is she talking about with that "toaster" stuff?' Adam asked.

Lee answered quite calmly, 'Captain Lescal is bigoted against synthetic life forms. She does not like androids, and does not approve of us taking a place in society.'

Adam almost choked. 'Android? Like a robot? You're an android?'

Lee seemed almost pleased by his reaction. 'You did not recognise that I was an android? I shall take that as a compliment.'

'But don't use the word "robot" for androids again,' Helena advised Adam. 'They generally don't like it.'

'Thank you,' Lee said graciously.

'*De nada*,' Helena answered. She waved the survivors out of the escape pod. 'Come with me, I'm a doctor. I'll give you all the once-over when we're safely in the shuttle.' The ragged group began to stagger out onto the uneven ground.

'I'll give you a hand,' Adam said, following Helena towards the most unsteady of the survivors.

'We should also return to the shuttle,' Erimem said. Her eyes were focused on the trees around them and the ominous darkness caused by the dense canopy of leaves above. 'The wildlife can see its prey escaping. That may cause the beasts to become bolder.'

Lescal pulled her blaster defiantly. 'Then I'll kill them.'

The refugees from the escape pod had reached the shuttle and disappeared inside. Movements began in the darkness all around the clearing.

'Can you kill all of them?' Erimem asked.

'If I have to.'

Erimem gave a snort of irritation and she turned her attention to Lee. 'Does your scout ship have, what is it called in films...? Yes! A tractor beam. Do you have a tractor beam?'

Lee frowned and ran through possible meanings for the unfamiliar term. She found a meaning in her memory banks. 'No,' she answered, 'we don't have a gravity beam but we do have a grapple. 'Why?'

Erimem nodded at the escape pod. 'Your ship might not be able to land but it may be able to use this pod to lower a rescue party to the other pods.' She turned to Lescal. 'Or would you rather walk ten kilometres through the forest trying not to be eaten?'

The undergrowth moved ominously. A rumble from deep in a large animal's throat rolled towards them.

Lee made the decision. 'It would take four or five hours to get through this kind of vegetation to the next pod. The shuttle can do it in a few minutes. I will have my troops attach the grapple to this pod and then we will be under way.'

'Oh, my, it's cold.'

Andy felt a pang of guilt and reached into the hood of the jacket Olivia was wearing and pressed a small button. Immediately the jacket began to warm. 'I asked one of the troopers why they weren't freezing their bollocks off. He showed me the thermal controls.'

Olivia shook herself and then relaxed considerably as the jacket, over-trousers and boots responded to the instructions and started to warm her. 'Actually, this is rather nice,' she said.

'Better than freezing our tits off,' Andy grinned.

Olivia blew her a playful kiss. 'It would take much longer to freeze yours than mine.'

Andy followed Olivia through the shuttle's open hatch into the blizzard outside. 'That's right. Make fun of the girl with big knockers.'

'I'm allowed to,' Olivia's voice came through Andy's earpiece. 'You're *my* girl with big knockers.'

Tom Niven's voice crackled self-consciously in their ears. 'And you're both on a public channel,' he said quietly. There was nothing malicious or unkind in his tone. If anything he seemed to be genuinely trying to be nice.

'Arse biscuits,' Andy muttered. 'Sorry everybody.'

Lieutenant Cade, who had been placed in command of this mission, crackled over the earpieces. 'Glad I'm not the only one with that problem, Andy,' she said. 'Let's move out.'

Cade deployed two of her troops to the front of their column to choose their path and dropped two to the back to guard their rear. The other five along with Cade, Andy, Olivia and Tom were in the central pack. Each of them, including the civilians, carried a weapon as well as cold weather clothing for whoever had survived.

The first of the escape pods had come down only a kilometre and a half from the place they had landed. The ground underfoot was naturally uneven but the several centimetres of snow resting on it made walking treacherous and slowed them down. The only positive to the heavy snow and biting winds was that it appeared to have sent the local wildlife into whatever den it called home.

After a quarter of an hour, Olivia nudged Andy and pointed at Tom. His arms were folded across his chest and each gust of wind seemed to take a toll on him.

Andy understood immediately. There was a temptation in her to leave him to it, a final little revenge for what he had done to Sasha.

No, she wasn't that much of a bitch. Whatever he had done, it couldn't change how she would act.

'Tom,' she said, toggling to a private channel, 'I'm guessing they forgot to tell you how to turn on the heat in your suit. Button inside the hood. Press it once and you'll be toasty in minutes.'

'Really?' Christ, he sounded like his teeth were chattering.

'Five minutes and you'll think you're on the beach in the Bahamas,' she assured him.

'Thanks.' She heard him press the button. A moment later she heard relief in his voice. 'Oh, that's better.' There was a brief pause before he spoke again. 'Thanks, Andy. I really appreciate that. Thank you.'

It was the most honest and heartfelt thing she had heard him say. Maybe there was hope for the git after all.

'No worries,' she said. 'Helena would go ape if I let you freeze on your first trip for a while.'

'Thanks, though.'

The march through the blizzard was completed remarkably quickly. The first escape pod was found with three survivors sitting inside, sheltering from the cold. They had almost exhausted the pod's limited supplies and were close to tears of relief when the rescue party arrived. They were all keen to tell their stories but Cade quieted them with a promise that Captain Watson would want to hear everything once they were aboard ship.

One of the pod's passengers had injured his leg on landing, so Cade left two of the troops to guard the little party, and to be collected on the way back to the shuttle. Settling into the warmth of the escape pod, the two marines chosen looked as they had won the Lottery and cheerfully waved goodbye to their comrades.

The next pod was only two kilometres further on. Four healthy adults looked at their rescuers with shock and relief. They gratefully accepted the thermal suits and joined the trek to the third pod in the area. There was no rescue to be had there. Half of the pods thrusters had failed to fire and it had slammed into the ground travelling far too fast for anyone to survive. The pod had cracked open on impact and the six bodies inside had already been stripped to the bone by local predators. A bone was taken from the hand of each of the skeletons so that they could be identified by DNA.

The last of the four pods Cade had been tasked with recovering was a kilometre further on. The majority of the forest they had travelled through was relatively thin by comparison with the rest of the planet, as if the weather wouldn't allow too much to flourish this close to the pole, but the pod had found a thicker clump of trees and looked as if its thrusters had charred a few on the way down.

The pod's hatch opened as they drew closer and the young woman inside waved to them desperately. 'Hurry,' she hissed. 'They're watching you. Hurry.'

The terror in the woman's voice had the party moving fast before Cade gave the order to run.

'Who's watching?' Andy demanded as they reached the pod.

The young woman was looking past the troops. 'Them,' she said.

Andy turned and saw the huge, shaggy creatures lowering themselves from the branches of trees. Their fur was thick and white, their eyes dark and merciless like a shark's. Their teeth would have been at home in a Great White, too. Raised up on their hind legs, thy must have been all of three metres tall. 'Shit!' was all she could think to say.

The seats in the escape pod were surprisingly comfortable. The journey Erimem had in the seat was considerably less appealing.

The grapple had bonded on a molecular level with the outside of the pod's hull. When that was secure Lescal had marched out and taken a seat inside the pod.

'I had planned for people to board it when we found the next escape pod,' Lee had said.

Erimem had simply shrugged and followed Lescal out into the pod.

'I'm a doctor,' Helena said and followed. 'That pod has a baby in it. I'm going as well.'

Lees' hand across his chest had stopped Adam following. 'Three idiots is enough.'

The shuttle was closed and secured, and the engines brought online. With something between a whine and a roar, the shuttle slowly began rising into the air. As it went, the tether line to the pod went taut and the pod began to move.

Enraged or emboldened by the sight of its prey escaping, a beast with a body the size of a bear but with eight muscular legs jointed like those of a spider, sped from the darkness beneath the trees and threw itself at the pod. The powerful legs scrabbled and clawed at the smooth surface, trying to prise the batch open. Hungry, bulbous eyes focused on them through the thick window and the beast clawed at the pod's hull all the harder.

The passengers were pushed back in their chairs as the pod was dragged along for a few metres then yanked off the ground as the shuttle rose more quickly, lifting the pod underneath it. The creature clung desperately to the pod, clawing at the window.

'Can it get in?' Erimem asked.

'Doubt it,' Helena answered, though she didn't sound convinced.

'Don't worry,' Lescal said. 'We're just clearing the trees.'

As soon as the shuttle was above the level of the tree-tops the main thrusters on the bottom of the ship increased power, taking the ship up more quickly. The blast buffeted the pod, but barely scorched the heat shielding. The eight-legged creature attacking the pod fared less well. The downward blast of the engines killed it instantly and sent it tumbling through the trees to the ground far below where its own kind fell upon it, tearing at the flesh and devouring it.

The shuttle moved forward at a measured pace with the pod dangling beneath it, skimming above the tops of the trees. The pod swung at the end of the cable. Lescal operated controls and the pod's thrusters fired short blasts, preventing the little craft from spinning.

Peering out of the pod's windows, they caught several glimpses of movement among the upper branches of the trees. There was no doubt that these forests were full of potentially aggressive life.

Lieutenant Commander Lee's voice cracked in their ear-pieces. 'We will be over the next pod in thirty seconds. Stand by to be lowered.'

'Understood,' Lescal answered.

A minute later the pod's interior was darkening as the pod was lowered through the canopy of leaves towards the ground. Dark shapes moved in the branches, shadows too indistinct to see clearly.

Broken branches and scorch marks marked the path the target

pod had taken, coming in at a slight angle through the trees. The pod was on the ground leaning against the thickest tree in the area. A deep gouge on the bark showed that the tree had slid down its side with a considerable force.

'The hatch is still closed,' Lescal said. She was craning her neck to see the ground below.

'That's good,' Helena said. She had managed to pull together a few minor pieces of first aid equipment but nothing even close to a medical kit.

The pod hit the ground and Lescal reached for the hatch release mechanism.

Erimem caught her hand. 'Wait,' she said, peering into the dark. 'There are creatures nearby.'

'How near?' Helena asked.

'I can't say.'

Lescal released the doors. 'Cover me.' She ran the few metres to the nearby pod.

'You stay here,' Erimem told Helena 'I will be with her.'

Lescal had already reached the other pod. She had drawn her blaster but her attention was entirely focused on opening the pod.

Erimem hurried the few metres to join her. Between them, she and Helena had a three hundred and sixty degree view around them. Unfortunately, that view was mostly of a darkness which shook and rustled with the movements of animals.

'No!'

Erimem turned at Lescal's anguished cry. 'What is it?'

Lescal stepped away from the pod. 'He's not there.' She sounded broken. 'He wasn't in the pod. This was the one the read-outs said he was in.'

'He was,' Erimem said.

Lescal didn't want to hear what she had to say. 'What did he do? Open the hatch and let himself out?'

Erimem grabbed Lescal and turned her around to face a screen beneath which a light flashed. Erimem had already pressed the button bringing the screen to life.

TOO DANGEROUS TO STAY HERE. BIG
ANIMALS. TOOK BABY TO MY POD.
1KM UP HILL. SAFER POSITION.

'The baby survived the landing,' Erimem said. 'They would

not have taken it otherwise.'

'That makes sense,' Helena agreed.

Lescal was looking around, trying to locate the hill. 'I can't see a damn thing for these trees.'

Lee's voice crackled in their ears. 'I have been monitoring your conversation. Return to your pod immediately.'

'Not without my nephew!' Lescal snarled.

Lee's voice came back calmly. 'You are surrounded by more than a dozen animals. They are organised, probably pack hunters. Return to your pod. I do not have time to deploy marines to rescue you.'

'Get your arses in here,' Helena shouted. 'I can see them in the shadows.'

Lescal was the best part of a head taller than Erimem but the smaller woman pushed her into the pod and Helena sealed the hatch.

The pod shook as a riot of animals slammed into the side of the pod. Teeth and claws flashed by the windows. Dark, dark blood smeared the outside of the window. As the predators fought each other to get to the pod.

'We are inside,' Erimem shouted. 'Get us away from here.'

The pod jolted as the shuttle lifted upwards. The three passengers were thrown into chairs and clung on as the pod crashed up through the branches.

'Shit a brick,' Helena said. 'They're coming after us.'

Through the windows they could see dark bestial shapes climbing the trees with a terrifying speed.

The pod burst into sunlight leaving the trees below. Claws soared from the trees towards them as one of the predators leaped from the highest branches of the trees. The claws scraped the outside of the pod, desperately pawing for some kind of purchase. There was nothing on the smooth surface for it to grip and with a sickening howl, the beast slid down the side of the pod and plummeted back towards the trees and the ground far below.

'Hurry,' Lescal said. 'If those things know where the other pod is... just hurry.'

'Increasing speed,' Lee's calm voice came back. The passengers clutched the restraints and hung on to their seats until

Lee's voice sounded again. Coming down now. The pod is on a ledge. I suggest to take care over your footing.'

Lescal snorted. 'She almost sounds concerned.'

Helena heaved herself up in her chair. 'There's no "almost" there. The concern is genuine.'

'Genuine?' Lescal snorted. 'Machines don't have emotions.'

'They can hear you, though,' Helena rebuked her sharply, 'and you know damn well we're on an open channel.'

'Great,' Lescal muttered. 'A machine lover.'

The pod bumped to a stop. Erimem looked through the windows before telling Lescal it was safe to open the hatch. The ledge which now housed two pods was thirty or more metres above ground level. It ran a good fifty metres in length, angling downwards, but was only five or six metres wide. Behind the first pod, a sheer cliff face rose for forty or fifty metres. Plants and more trees hung over the edge high above them. The ground below their feet was spongy, with some moss-like growth covering the rocks. Broken branches were strewn across the moss.

Lescal went straight for the pod. 'Alex? Alex? Have you got Alex in there?'

Erimem peered through the glass into the pod. 'It's empty,' she said.

Lescal keyed in the override and impatiently heaved he hatch open. The interior showed signs of having been inhabited by a single person. Two seats had been turned into a bed, and a food-pack and water were discarded on a control console.

'How long has she been gone?' asked Helena.

Lescal consulted the pod's log. 'About eighteen hours. They could be anywhere in the area. I assume the metal-head is listening?'

'I am,' Lee answered, 'but I would ask you to refrain from using that term. I do find it offensive.'

'Yeah, I'll remember that,' Lescal said sarcastically.

Erimem was peering intently at the log's display on the screen. 'You are wrong,' she said to Lescal. She tapped the display, her finger picking out the time display. 'The message in the other pod was written only three hours ago. They cannot have gone far in just three hours, especially in this environment with so many of these predators around.'

Helena agreed. 'So they're most likely somewhere between here and that other pod.'

'Yes,' Erimem nodded.

Helena's face was grave. 'Three hours is a long time even to get through this jungle.'

'They'd have had to hide a lot,' Lescal said. 'Maybe take detours to avoid being caught. It's possible.' She started towards the ledge's downwards slope.

'Wait,' Lee's voice crackled.

'Go to hell.'

Six metal poles rained down, perfectly vertically. A marine, attached to the pole by their belts, slid quickly down each pole, slowing only when they were a few metres from the ground. As soon as they stepped off, a second soldier slid down each from the shuttle to the ground.Lee was among them.

'We will find your nephew quicker if we have more teams searching,' Lee said. She spoke to her marines. 'Five teams of three, standard Beta search pattern. Take no chances. If these animals attack, shoot to kill. Stay alert, find the boy, get back here.' She pointed quickly to Erimem and Helena. 'You two are with me.'

The path down the slope showed markings of footprints going only one way. As the slope curved out in the rough direction of the abandoned pod, the teams split, straying no further than five metres from the next team on the outward leg of the search. That would spread if necessary.

Tracking had been a skill at which Erimem prided herself in showing more than average proficiency. At home in Thebes, Antranak, her beloved mentor, had taught her many of the arts of war, but tracking had been one from which she had taken a great deal of satisfaction. It was a puzzle, a challenge, to find clues left behind and obscured either by time and the weather or by a cunning enemy. Antranak had once said "With tracking skills like these, at least you will always have the chance to find someone to fight so that you can show off the skills I taught you." And there was no doubt he had taught her well. Unfortunately, the tactical display on what looked like a tablet carried by Lee, was designed to track footprints, broken leaves and branches and everything else she had learned. It was remarkable, wonderful machine, and it made her feel redundant in tracing this infant. Erimem hated the thought that she might be obsolete or simply useless because her skills were out of date. It was one of the reasons she was obsessed with learning about everywhere she travelled.

She did have to admit that the tablet's tracking software was quite exceptional, though it didn't have the subtlety to point out when the girl from the pod had been on her toes, which Erimem knew usually meant that she had been running. Halfway between the pods they found a churned piece of ground which showed that the girl had come back this way from the pod. The tracks were unmistakable – she had been running and she had been chased by, well, who knew what had been chasing her but there had been several of them. She had veered away from the outward path, arrowing in towards a cliff face. The ground at the cliff face had been trampled and scratched by heavy clawed feet but there was no sign of blood on the ground. Had the woman and the child been carried away to be devoured later?

Erimem dropped to her knees and looked at a slab of stone which leaned against the cliff face. 'Weather eroded the cliff and caused this to shear off.'

'So?' Lescal was understandably agitated. 'How does that help me find me nephew?'

Erimem ran a hand over the stone, wiping a layer of dust away. 'Is it likely to have fallen upright this way? Surely it is more likely to have toppled or shattered.'

'You don't think it belongs there?' Helena asked.

'In Egypt we used stones to cover the entrances to our tombs,' Erimem answered, 'to *hide* them.' She picked up a small stone and tapped the large slab three times. She waited a moment then tapped three times again. She finished her third set of taps when a reply came from the other side of the slab. Three gentle, tentative taps.

Lee waved her men forward. 'Move that.'

Two men heaved the stone slab aside. A young woman peered out of a natural hollow eroded under the face of the cliff. It wasn't big enough to be a cave but that lack of size was what had stopped the predators following.

'Do you have the baby there?' Lescal demanded. 'He's my nephew. Is he in there?'

The woman slid out from the tiny alcove and reached behind to pluck out the baby. 'He's hungry. I've nothing to give him.'

'Give him to me.' Lescal took the baby from the girl. She inspected the baby carefully. 'Is he hurt?'

'Let me see,' Helena said, reaching for the child. Lescal was reluctant to let him go, but Helena managed to ease him into her arms. She gave him a quick once–over. 'Other than hungry and tired he seems to be fine.' She winced and pulled a face. 'He could use a change, though.'

'They're back.'

All eyes turned to the girl who had been protecting baby Alex.

'Who are?' asked Lee.

'The monsters,' Lee answered. 'I don't know what else to call them.'

'What is your name?' Erimem demanded.

'Nessa,' the girl answered.

'Well, Nessa,' Lee took over, 'get ready to run. We're going back to your escape pod. Our ship will pick us up there.'

'We'll never make it,' Nessa said simply. 'There's too many of them. They don't stop. Bring your ship here.'

Lee slapped the cliff face at the pointed at the trees. It would never get in here. Don't worry. We have fifteen guns here. We'll get back.'

Reluctantly, Lescal handed baby Alex back to Nessa 'I'm more use with a gun in my hand. Look after my nephew.'

Nessa was right. The creatures that had tracked her had indeed returned. They stayed out of sight, following the marine party as they ran back towards the ledge. The trees began to move. Darkly shadowed braches shook; animal snarls and breathing came from all around.

The party of soldiers moved quickly and efficiently, sticking to their trusted formation. The first scent of an attack came when one of the eight legged creatures they had encountered earlier moved out into the dim light. It paused, gathering itself and they ran across the uneven ground with terrifying speed. Shots to the head and the legs took the creature down. Before it could stand, others of its kind were on it, teeth and claws ripping at the stricken creature. It screamed in pain and rage as its legs were torn free and its huge body ravaged by the blood-fuelled frenzy of the others. Great chunks of the screaming beast's flesh were turn away and eaten as it thrashed its last.

The vile attack had bought the fleeing humans the time to run fifty metres but the bloodlust had now fallen on the creatures of the forest. Two more of the creatures fell under the troopers' gunfire and were immediately being torn apart by teeth and claws but the forest was full of predators, not only the eight legged giants but smaller animals the size of a dog which had tentacles writhing around mouths full of needle sharp teeth. The sounds of the creatures feeding had roused every animal in the forest, and every animal in the forest was hungry.

'Run!' Erimem yelled. 'Run!'

The soldiers ran.

The snow was dark with blood. Andy could barely bring herself to believe that none of it belonged to her.

The attack of those whatever-the hell-they-were had only just been repelled. She had put two shots straight into the head of one and it had kept coming. It was only when she fired into its open maw that the beast finally toppled, dead.

'Any ideas?' Andy asked Lieutenant Cade.

'Does prayer count?'

Andy couldn't help but smile. It was the sort of answer she would give. Jesus, she thought, she must have been annoying to talk with sometimes. How did Olivia and Erimem put up with her?

'I was hoping for something more substantial and rousing,' she answered. 'Maybe a bit of military genius?'

Cade shrugged. 'I missed the military genius class. Hangover.'

Yep, Cade was all right. Always trust a boozer. The pod caught Andy's eye. 'What about the thrusters?' she asked. 'Could they be turned into a weapon of some sort? A flame-thrower maybe?'

Cade thought for a moment before reluctantly shaking her

head. They're too big to detach and carry and it would take days to remove them safely.'

'Could they be made into a cannon?' Olivia asked. 'Have them fire rocks at those monsters? Large enough to cause damage but small and sharp enough to cut their flesh.'

'Blood-thirsty bunch, aren't you?' Cade muttered. 'I suppose we could do that but when we were out of fuel we'd still be here and surrounded by dead or really angry monsters.'

For the first time, Tom made a suggestion. 'Could we use it to kick up the snow so that we could get away? You know? Like a dust-storm only snow.'

'They're used to seeing through snow,' Cade said. 'I do have a thought though.' She clambered into the pod and peered at the controls. 'It's still got a little juice left.'

'Could we all fit in it?' Andy asked.

'There aren't enough seats,' one of the survivors protested.

'Sod the seats, we'll stand,' Andy said.

'It might just have enough to get us back to the shuttle,' Cade said.

Andy shook her head. 'But we're not going to the shuttle. We've got to pick up the first set of survivors, remember?'

'Damn,' Cade cursed. 'So we do.' She looked at Andy hopefully. 'I don't suppose you've ever piloted one of these things, have you?'

'Oh, this is going to be fun,' Andy grumbled.'

'All right,' Cade yelled, 'inside the pod, everybody. I don't care how uncomfortable it is. Just get in.'

Normally Erimem disliked guns. They were a brutal, personality-less weapon. It was better to see who and what you were killing. Taking life should never be easy. That was why she preferred swords or her khopesh daggers. In this case, she made an exception. Beasts swarmed from the trees and undergrowth. The marines picked them off, one or two shots killing each beast but more kept coming. Every death excited their senses them more.

The first marine to fall was taken as the group reached the curve up onto the slope towards the pod. He was defending the rear of the fleeing pack. What looked like a cross between a gorilla and a bear leaped on him from the trees, covering an absurd distance in one bound. He managed to loose one shot into the furry hide but it didn't slow the animal. Its huge hands caught each side of his head and twisted, ripping it from his shoulders. The head was hurled aside and the beast began devouring the bloodied neck.

The fleeing group ran all the faster at the sight of their fallen comrade being eaten. Erimem turned her weapon on the Trees at the bottom of the slope. Animals abandoned the branches attacking each other as they fled.

'What the hell are you doing?' Lescal asked.

A tree cracked and splintered, toppling so that it fell across the slope.

'She's buying us time,' Helena snapped. She opened fire, bringing down another tree on top of Erimem's. Adam brought a third tree down.

'Can you make them burn? Erimem demanded.

Lescal adjusted her blaster and opened fire on the trees. She blasted along the length of the fallen trees, watching flames sprout from the bark and the branches. Animals screeched and pulled back from the sudden inferno.

'It is unlikely to hold them for long,' Erimem said.

'Hopefully, long enough,' Lee answered. She urged her troops up the slope. 'Hurry. We don't have much time.'

Erimem watched Lee. Before the First Officer turned and ran up the slope, her last look was back towards where her soldier was being eaten. There as the pain of an officer losing one of her troops on her face just for a moment. Did the machine-woman actually *feel*? That was something she would discuss with Helena and Andy later.

For now it was just important to *run*.

CHAPTER EIGHT

'Fuck-fuck-fuck-fuck-fuck-fuck-fuuuuuck!'

The escape pod dropped the last few metres, landing hard in the snow. In the cramped little craft's interior, the troops and refugees from the *Andromedan Princess* were thrown about violently as the pod came to a sudden stop.

'Anybody hurt?' Andy shouted.

There were moans and complaints but no-one seemed to be badly injured.

'What the hell happened?' Lieutenant Cade asked.

'We ran out of fuel,' Andy answered. 'This thing's not built for taking off – especially with so many people aboard. It was almost wiped out by just taking off. We're lucky to have got here in one piece.'

Cade inspected the area outside of the pod through the small window. 'We're clear to go,' she said. 'We missed the other pod by about ten metres. That's something, I suppose.'

'Everybody's a critic,' Andy muttered.

Olivia kissed the top of her head. 'You got us away from those animals. I think they will forgive you for the rough way we came ashore.'

Andy pushed herself upright and winced. 'I'm not sure my back will. That was a bad landing.'

Olivia took her hand and pulled her after the crowd that had spilled out onto the snow. 'When we get back to the ship I will kiss it better for you.'

'Are you just using sex to motivate me?'

Olivia smiled innocently. 'Yes.'

Andy shrugged. 'You know what? I'm okay with that.'

'I thought you would be.'

Cade had already collected the marines and passengers who had been waiting in the warmth of the other pod. 'Okay,' she said, 'this isn't a long trek but it has to be a quick one. You all know what's in these woods. If you're armed, be ready to fire. If you're not armed, keep your eyes peeled and shout if you see anything. Now form up and let's get moving.'

Enough snow had fallen in the short time they had been away to smooth the edges of their footprints, making the snow look like rippling white sand.

Around the party, trees rustled and branches creaked. Occasional animal sounds came but they seemed to be quite distant.

The party hurried on through the blizzard.

A scrabbling sound from the side of the sloping path up to the shuttle told Erimem that their escape was not secure yet. The edge of the path dropped away in a sheer rock face. Animals from the forest were swarming up the rough stone. Their claws found crevices and holds letting them move with a horrifying speed. The nearest was barely two metres away. Two shots from Erimem's blaster sent it tumbling down the cliff, knocking other animals below it loose. They all landed hard and fought among themselves but the least injured were climbing again almost immediately.

Lee had joined her at the edge and blasted two of the beasts. 'A-squad get the civilians up to the shuttle. B-Squad here with me. We'll hold these at bay and give you as much time as possible.'

Six troopers split from the main group and ran to the side of the ledge. On Lee's order they opened fire, blasting downwards. They spread out, trying to cover as much of the climb as they could. There were too many of the beasts swarming up the cliff, screeching their blood lust.

Lescal took command of urging the civilian survivors up towards the six metal poles which were still suspended from the hovering shuttle. Lescal's eyes focused on Nessa, who was still carrying a screeching Alex. 'You're in the first batch to go up,' she told Nessa. 'Hold my nephew tight and don't let go.'

Nessa nodded and ran. She had made half a dozen steps before her knees buckled. An eight legged bear had broken the cordon at the ledge. One of its muscular legs had caught the ankle of a marine and swept him over the edge. His screams were ended as he was caught mid-fall and torn apart by the animals on the cliff face.

Nessa was closest to the enraged beast. It lashed out and struck the back of her knees causing her to topple hard to the ground. She managed to twist as she fell so that she didn't land on the baby. She tried to push herself upright. The powerful leg slashed down again. This time a claw emerged from its tip and speared hard into Nessa's thigh. She was dragged towards the huge animal. Its mouth opened, teeth bared... and the front of its head exploded in a mass of bone and blood and fur. Lescal fired again, turning its brain to spray.

Nessa whimpered and tried to move but she was pinned by the weight of that giant leg. She had pulled Alex close and sheltered him under her body. She screamed when Lescal tried to pull the leg free.

'Damn!' Lescal held one of the animal's other legs briefly before throwing it side. 'There's a barb on the end of the claw. I'll rip your leg open if I pull it out.' She aimed her blaster and shot through the animal's leg about thirty centimetres from Nessa's leg. She heaved the girl upright and pressed the baby tighter into her grasp. 'You'll be fine once you're on the shuttle. Damn it!'

The curse was caused by the sight of six civilians heading upwards towards the shuttle which hovered around thirty metres above. The small discs at the base of the poles acted as platforms to stand on and the magnetic belts kept the civilians from flailing as they ascended into the shuttle.

'Get those lifters back down here ASAP,' Lescal yelled.

Nessa hobbled painfully at her side. She could scarcely put any weight on her injured leg. The baby's screams cut through Lescal. She was supposed to be a soldier, damn it. She should be defending their retreat. She was also looking after her family.

Lee and her troops were falling back. They had lost the battle to hold the edge of the precipice. There were just too many animals of so many shapes and sizes, swarming up over the side of the ledge. The marines formed a line, sending a relentless stream of fire at these monsters, but they were still in danger over being overrun at any moment.

Lescal had looked away for just an instant to take in the situation of the marines. That was enough. A mass of hair and teeth slammed into Lescal, knocking her flat on her back. Her head struck a rock as she fell and she saw that Nessa had also been knocked to the ground. A small ape-like creature ripped Alex from Nessa's arms and was gone from her sight. Lescal tries to right herself but another blow from one of the creatures to the side of her head sent her into darkness.

Erimem knew that the battle was lost. As good as the marines were, the animals were just too numerous for them and would overwhelm them. Lee hadn't wanted to listen when Erimem had said they would have to pull back but she saw the sense. If they didn't draw back now they would be cut off from their way back to the shuttle.

'Hold a steady line,' Erimem shouted to Adam and Helena.

'Not my first rodeo,' Helena called back, firing two shots that tore a leg from a dog-sized animal.

'Damn!'

'What is it?' Erimem asked Lee. Lee didn't answer. Erimem loosed three shots then glanced to why Lee hadn't answered.

Lee wasn't there.

Erimem turned and saw Lee running hard after some kind of small primate which what holding the baby they had come to save. 'Close the line!' Erimem shouted. 'Tighten the gaps! I'll be back!' She didn't wait to hear a reply. Instead she turned and ran after Lee.

Ibrahim Hadmani was having a rather relaxing day. The trips through the jungle had been remarkably incident free. There had been a few roars from various animals but the escape pods they were rescuing had all come down in areas open enough for the shuttle to land so the furthest he'd had to trek was about forty metres. Settling into his seat, Ibrahim secured the buckle in place. He hoped the others were finding their rescues as easy.

'Adam, drop back and get Lescal and Nessa to those lift things.'

It didn't occur to Adam Docherty that he shouldn't do as he was instructed. Holstering his weapon he ran to the fallen women. Nessa was hurt badly. The clawed leg embedded in her thigh would cripple her, and she had two gouges in her side. She would go into shock from blood loss soon. Lescal looked concussed. Her eyes were open but unfocused. Getting her up that Bat-pole contraction to the shuttle would be difficult. Somebody would have to go up with her.

'Come on,' he said. 'You're going up to the shuttle.'

He tried to lift her but she weakly pushed him away. 'Alex,' she slurred. 'Get Alex.'

Adam ignored Lescal's protests and dragged her to the little group waiting at the bottom of the landing poles. 'Do not let her move!' he shouted before running back to Nessa. She was barely conscious and he had to carry her to Lescal's side. In the time he had been away, the poles had become ready for use. 'These two are going to need helped to stay on. Somebody has to go on with them. Understood?'

Lescal tried weakly to fight her way free of the hands helping her to safety. 'Nephew,' she managed to blurt. 'My nephew.'

A small, screaming bundle was pushed into Lescal's arms. 'Hold them both tightly, Lieutenant Commander Lee ordered, before turning away and returning to the fight. Lee was scarred across the cheek and forehead and her uniform was ripped badly. Erimem was also coated in blood which made Adam's stomach lurch but she was moving freely back into battle at Lee's side. Adam drew his sidearm and followed suit.

The yomp through the snow back to the shuttle had been pleasingly dull. Andy, Olivia and Tom had stayed with the rescued holidaymakers, cajoling them to keep up and even nudging and pushing when the pace started to drop.

They were around thirty metres from the shuttle when the darkness among the trees started to come alive.

'They've been waiting,' Andy muttered. 'Everybody move faster.'

Lieutenant Cade was on her radio to the shuttle. 'Open the hatch and get every gun ready. We're almost there but the locals are getting restless. Give us cover if we need it.'

The shuttle's hatch slid open.

Vicious snarling beasts erupted from the darkness. The air was filled with searing bolts of energy. Every marine blasted a non-stop stream of fire at the screeching animals.

The gunfire kept the animals at bay long enough for the party to reach the shuttle. The rescued holiday makers were hurried through the hatch while the marines laid down covering fire.

A six legged animal the size of a large dog broke through the wall of fire and slammed into Olivia. She staggered backwards, taking Andy to the ground with her. Sharp, angry teeth reached for Olivia's throat...

...and the side of the animal's head exploded.

Tom fired a second shot into the animal just to be sure.

Andy was already helping Olivia to her feet. They scrambled into the shuttle and the marines followed. Cade released a final shot before she was last aboard.

'Get us up!' Cade yelled.

The shuttle shook as a torrent of enraged animals slammed into it. Claws and teeth scraped at the hull. The sound of the engines rising finally drowned out the attack from outside and the shuttle lifted off, rising quickly into the air. The last claws scraped the outside of the hung as the animals that had clung to the ship slid down its hull and fell to the ground far below.

As soon as they were off the ground Andy turned to Olivia. 'Are you hurt? Did it bite you? What about its claws? Are you okay?'

'I am fine,' Olivia reassured her. 'The beast just took the breath from me.'

'You're not hurt? You're sure?'

Olivia kissed Andy hard. 'I'm fine. I'm not hurt.'

Andy sank back into her seat in relief. She turned to the next seat where Tom Niven sat catching his breath. 'Thank you,' she said.

Tom nodded. 'It's cool.'

She squeezed his arm briefly. 'Thank you.'

For the first time, Andy got past her animosity towards Tom. She was just grateful that he had shot the animal before it had hurt Olivia.

'Thanks,' she said again.

Tom nodded and smiled self-consciously.

Andy slipped her hand into Olivia's and sank back into her seat.

'We have a problem,' Erimem said to Lee.

Lee blasted the nearest animal twice. 'That is an understatement.'

Erimem kept up a constant fire. The weapon was now painfully hot to hold. 'Those lifting columns can take six – twelve at most. That would still leave a small number on the ground here.'

'I will stay behind with three of my troops,' Lee said evenly. 'You and your friends should go on the next uplifts.'

'That would leave you and your soldiers to die.'

'We will hold out as long as we can,' Lee answered.

Erimem fired another volley. An idea was forming in her head. It was absurd, stupid and dangerous. It was all she could think of. 'Drop your men back to the lifters. You will join us in the escape pod.' She saw the understanding in Lee's face.

The First Officer relayed the instructions. The troops fell back firing a constant barrage of energy bolts at the animals. As the six lifters rose Erimem, Helena, Adam and Lee released a final volley of fire before throwing themselves into the escape pod. The hatch slid shut just in time. A moment later the first of the wild beasts slammed into the pod. The interior went dark as fur and teeth and claws swarmed the outside of the pod. Lee threw switches bringing the power online. The main lights flickered to life and the pod's limited systems hummed with power.

'This is Lieutenant Commander Lee. Lift the pod immediately.'

Helena added her voice. 'She means get us out of here now!'

The pod lurched and the four occupants struggled to fasten their belts. Still attached to the shuttle by the tether line, the pod suddenly and violently swung forward. Increasing pace as it moved, the pod was a wrecking ball, smashing its way through the animals, scattering them and sending a dozen or more over the precipice. The winch holding the tether line began to reel the pod in. Abruptly, the pod began to shake under the onslaught of blaster fire.

'Hey,' Helena yelled, 'calm down. We're on the same side, remember?'

One of the eight legged bears fell fast a window.

'Don't worry,' Erimem said. 'They are just getting all of the animals off of the outside of the pod.'

'As long as they don't shoot the tether,' Helena muttered. 'I didn't get to be this old just to die playing conkers with that lot out there?'

'Conkers?' Lee asked. 'What is conkers? And why do you say you are old? You appear to be no more than your early thirties.'

'They're both older than they look.' That came from Adam.

Erimem scrutinised him but she couldn't decipher if that had been meant in fun or if his anger still had some roots left. In the end, she let it pass and relaxed as the pod was pulled to the shuttle and drawn into its cargo hold. As soon as they were secured, the pod was opened. Helena was whisked away to tend to Nessa and Lescal.

The shuttle left the atmosphere and joined the other three shuttles in their convoy towards The *Andromedan Princess* and the *Saint-Saens*. The two ships were still joined by the docking tube and despite their protests, when the rescued holidaymakers were safely on board the *Saint-Saens*, they were immediately transferred back to the *Andromedan Princess*.

Several decks of the liner were still sealed and on minimum power, but the passengers were able to be moved into quarters that had been empty during the voyage. Where possible their luggage had been retrieved while Helena and the *Saint-Saens'* medical team gave them a full examination.

Some of the marines had picked up injuries which required

treatment but the worst injuries among those who made it back to the ship were those collected by Lescal and Nessa. The girl's leg was so badly damaged that she would certainly have lost it without immediate treatment. The surgery to remove the barbed claw would take time and care. Lescal was diagnosed with a concussion and put into a deep sleep for at least twelve hours while her condition was monitored. An appalled junior ensign who had never held an infant in his life was given the duty of looking after baby Alex. He looked as if he would have been happier down on the planet facing a horde of wild animals.

Captain Watson convened a meeting to take reports on the rescue missions. The loss of marines clearly weighed on him. They were his men and women and his responsibility. The recovery of the civilians from such a hostile environment was far more of a cause for relief if not celebration. That they had recovered around thirty souls in total was hardly a huge success.

'Some have injuries,' Erimem told Watson, 'but they will heal quickly enough.'

'At least physically,' Andy added. 'Psychologically... that's likely to take longer.'

Erimem nodded her agreement. 'Each of them has lost family. They either know that their loved ones were... well, as we found them, or they are about to find out. That will not be easy for anyone.'

Watson sighed. 'I'll assign whatever medics they need until we get back to port and we can hand them across to the appropriate civilian authorities.'

'I am sure Helena will help as well,' Erimem said. 'She is working well with your medical team at the moment.'

The door slid open and a slightly unsteady-looking Lee entered. 'My apologies for being late, Captain,' she said. 'I had to visit the medics.' There were dressings covering the stitches on her cheek and forehead. Her left arm was held across her chest in a sling.'

'Are you fit for duty?' Watson asked. His voice had a slightly paternal tone rather than that of just a superior officer.

'I will recover fully,' Lee replied, though she looked relieved at being able to sit down.

Curiosity was written all across Andy's face. 'I'm really

sorry if this is an ignorant thing to ask. If it is, I really do apologise, but you are an android, right?'

'Yes,' Lee replied.

'But you went to the medic rather than...'

'Engineering?' Lee suggested. She seemed amused rather than offended. 'Should I have asked an electrician to repair me?'

Andy grimaced, looking slightly embarrassed at her own lack of knowledge. 'I just wondered if you would need a specialist to treat you.'

'You have never met an android, have you?' Lee asked.

Andy shook her head. 'Sorry. You are my first. Got to say, you're pretty incredible.'

'Thank you,' Lee said with a slight bow. 'Let me explain. Androids of my classification are not built on factory production lines. We are grown over a skeleton. Our tissue is a mixture of organic and mechanical at a cellular level. We are no longer the property of anyone. We free, independent and we control our own reproduction.'

'Good on you,' Andy said. 'More power to you.'

'Power?' Lee frowned. 'We absorb energy from food the same as you.' She smiled. 'Although if necessary we can recharge in more traditionally mechanical ways.'

'It's just a saying.' Andy's grin got wider. 'You're fantastic, and given how amazing my friends are, that's pretty high praise.'

'Thank you again,' Lee said. 'I also find one of your friends amazing,' she said, looking at Erimem. 'I have an interest in history. You have a remarkable similarity to someone who bore the same name.'

'Family,' Ibrahim said. 'We're from that same line.'

'Extraordinary,' Lee said, 'but absolutely fascinating.'

Andy waved a hand. 'For what it's worth, I'm absolutely nobody interesting.'

'Not true,' Olivia said softly. They touched fingers momentarily.

A smile of approval appeared at the corner of Lee's mouth.

A radio chimed for attention and the captain answered. 'Watson here.'

'There's a ship approaching, sir,' came the voice from the bridge. 'It's ignoring hails.'

'Let's see it,' Watson ordered.'

A monitor flashed to life, showing the grainy distant image of a sharp, angular red spaceship.

'Shit,' Andy said.

'Indeed,' Erimem agreed. 'Shit.'

Watson's eyes turned to them. 'You recognise it?'

Erimem nodded. 'It is a Drofen ship. Similar to the one we have seen before.'

'Only bigger,' Andy added, 'and it looks a shitload nastier. The one in Russia didn't have that many weapon-ports.'

'That is a warship,' Olivia agreed. 'Different than the kind I know but unmistakable.'

'How long till it gets here?' Watson demanded.

The bridge answered almost immediately. 'Seventeen minutes, sir.'

Watson rose to his feet. 'Get back to the liner. I'll leave you as much of a crew as I can spare but we'll need every man if we're going into battle.'

'Can the *Andromedan Princess* help in the fight?' Erimem asked.

'With no weapons and holes in her hull?' Watson shook his head. 'Withdraw and stay out of the action. Whatever happens, do not get involved.'

Erimem and Andy led their party back to the *Andromedan Princess*. Minutes later the docking tube was collapsed and the ships separated.

They were surprised to find how much progress had been made on repairing the ship's systems but shocked to see how small the crew they had been afforded was. Only the most junior members of the *Saint-Saens'* crew had been spared to keep the liner running and none of them was an officer.

'So they've left us with no captain?' Adam said. 'That's good of them.'

'I think we have to supply our own skipper,' Ibrahim said.

Helena shook her head. 'Don't look at me. I'm busy enough looking after the patients we rescued.'

'And I'm her glamorous sidekick,' Ibrahim added.

Erimem looked to Olivia. 'You are the only actual captain among us.'

'And if this was a sailing ship I should happily taker her wheel,' Olivia answered. 'I do not know these ships as well as others here.'

Andy threw Erimem a loose salute. 'She's all yours, skipper.' A young crewman moved aside to allow Andy access to a control console.

'All right,' Erimem said, 'who is our navigator?'

'I am,' a young woman said. She looked barely old enough to have left school.

'What is your name?' Erimem asked. 'Not your rank, your name.'

'Haniya,' the girl answered.

'Where is your family from? Where do they call home?'

Haniya looked slightly bemused by the conversation. 'Pakistan?'

Erimem smiled reassuringly at her. 'Haniya, just remember your training and follow orders and you will make your family in Pakistan very proud of you.'

'Yes, Captain,' Haniya said. She focused her eyes on the controls and waited for orders.

'Andy, what is our situation?' Erimem asked.

Andy was still scrolling through the displays in front of her. 'We've still got holes in our side but those decks are sealed by bulkheads and anyway they're covered by force-fields. The engines are up to full beans, life support is ticking over fine... it's all looking good.'

'Very well,' Erimem said. 'Haniya, drop us back two hundred kilometres from the *Saint-Saens*.'

Haniya input a series on commands and the ship's deckplates vibrated slightly as the liner began to move. 'Yes, ma'am.'

'Prepare two courses,' Erimem said, 'one that will take us back to the nearest safe base for us and the other...'

'Straight back into the fire,' Andy finished for her.

Haniya looked up sharply.

Erimem nodded. 'And the second to return to the *Saint-Saens*,' she confirmed. 'Be ready for either of those courses on my command.'

'Yes, ma'am.'

Erimem glanced at Andy. Somehow she had expected her

friend to make a flippant remark. It didn't come.

That made her just a bit nervous.

The Drofen cruiser approached the planet at high speed. The *Saint-Saens* sent repeated hails to the ship, requesting identification. Captain Watson left a communications channel open for the approaching ship to use. Nobody expected them to use it.

Watson spoked clearly. 'Unknown spacecraft, this is the battle cruiser *Saint-Saens*. We have recently rescued survivors of an unprovoked, unwarranted attack on a civilian ship. This is an ongoing military situation. Please slow your approach and we will share our information on the situation.'

The Drofen ship kept approaching. Its weapon ports registered as fully charged and its shielding went active.

Watson tried again, remaining as calm as possible. 'Unknown spaceship, please be aware that we are on maximum alert. We will not instigate any action but anyone who attacks us will face a severe and fatal retaliation. Please slow and we will discuss the situation.'

The Drofen opened fire. The red ship unleashed a beam of phased plasma. The *Saint-Saens*' protective shield held firm, dissipating the energy across its surface and absorbing it.

On Watson's order the *Saint-Saens* returned fire. Six turrets swivelled and fired volley after volley of pulsed energy at the red ship. The Drofen's response was merciless. Energy beams shot from a dozen emitters across the ship's surface. The *Saint-Saens* rocked under the attack. Its shields wavered, threatening to be overwhelmed by the attack. The warship adjusted its targeting and two of the emitters exploded. The other ten kept firing, pounding the *Saint-Saens*' shields.

On the viewscreen aboard the *Andromedan Princess*, the makeshift crew watched the battle impassively. Olivia's hand slid into Andy's.

The two battleships fired at each other relentlessly, trading massive blows. At times the lights on both ships flickered as they struggled to cope. Inevitably the shields on the two ships began to fail, first on the *Saint-Saens* and then on the Drofen ship. Gas or vapour of some kind began to vent from the Drofen ship.

'Fuel line,' Andy said automatically.

There was no time for celebration. A beam from the Drofen ship sheared through the *Saint-Saens'* hull, opening its interior to the vacuum. The energy sliced through the interior decks. Abruptly the *Saint-Saens* went dark.

'They're shot out the *Saint-Saens'* engines,' Andy reported. 'They're moving in to board.'

Erimem's eyes never left the screen. 'Does this ship have any weapons?' she asked.

'None,' Andy reported. 'Well, none but a few lasers to pick off any small asteroids in the way.'

'I need more than that,' Erimem snapped. The crew of the *Saint Saens* will not survive being boarded by the Drofen.' She stopped abruptly. 'Why do the lasers only deal with *small* asteroids?'

'Because they're small lasers?' Andy offered.

Erimem's head shook in irritation. 'What about larger asteroids? How does the ship deal with them?'

Andy shook her head, puzzled. 'Goes round them?' She looked at the display in front of her and had her epiphany. 'Or it uses some sort of deflector. Think I'm nicking that term from *Star Trek* but it's the best I can think of.'

'What does this deflector do?' Erimem asked. 'Other than deflect things obviously.'

Andy read the display. 'Sends a pulse wave of energy which deflects or destroys the asteroid.'

That was good enough for Erimem. 'Prepare to use this deflector,' she said. She glanced at Olivia. 'Have you ever rammed another ship?'

'Not deliberately.'

'Then today is a new experience.' She spoke to her navigator. 'Take us straight at the Drofen ship, as fast as you can manage.'

The young officer's hands tightened into fists for a moment but she obeyed the order. The two ships ahead began to loom larger on the viewscreen.

'Are our shields operating properly?' Erimem asked.

'I bloody hope so,' Andy muttered before answering, 'Maximum output.'

Erimem nodded. 'And the deflector?'

'Charged and ready to, well, deflect.'

Adam had positioned himself by a display screen. 'The Drofen are closing on the *Saint-Saens*.'

Erimem absorbed the information but didn't acknowledge it directly. 'How long till we intercept the Drofen?'

'Twenty seven seconds,' Haniya answered.

'Can we move any faster?'

'No,' Haniya said. 'We're still building acceleration.

'Will we reach them before they begin boarding the *Saint-Saens*?' Erimem pressed.

Haniya inspected her controls. 'Depends how the attack. If they dock we'll be there with seconds to spare. If they launch boarding shuttles they'll beat us to it.'

Erimem swore, an ancient Egyptian curse she hadn't used in millennia. 'Tell me when we are ten seconds from the ship and then again at five.' She glanced at Andy. 'Are you ready to use the deflector?'

'Ready,' Andy confirmed.'

'All right,' Erimem said, 'I have no idea how this will affect our ship but it may save our friends. Just hold on.'

'Ten seconds,' Haniya said.

Erimem counted in her head, ticking off the seconds.

Haniya spoke again. 'Five seconds.'

'Activate now, Andy,' Erimem said. 'Now.'

Andy's hand moved across the controls. 'Done.'

Nothing happened. There was no sound, no recoil, no sign at all that the ship had done anything.

Until two seconds later the Drofen ship was bucked as if it had been hit by a tsunami. It toppled and spun wildly as its thrusters struggled to control the spin, sending a spray of fuel in ridiculously random directions.

'Does anyone here think they could use the laser to hit the place the fuel is escaping?' Erimem asked.

'I'm firearms trained,' Adam said. He glanced at Tom. 'Unless...'

Tom shook his head. 'I'm the American who has never fired a gun.' He shrugged. 'On Earth anyway.'

'Okay, it's me, then.' Adam moved to the laser firing controls and familiarised himself with them. 'Okay. This is nothing like at Hendon.'

Erimem's eyebrow rose. 'Are you saying you can't do it?'

He waved a hand to buy some time. 'Give me a second or two.' He nodded to himself. 'It's nothing like I learned in the police but pretty much any gamer in the world could use this thing.'

'Then use it quickly,' Erimem said. 'They are bringing their ship under control.'

She was right. The Drofen ship's thrusters had almost stopped the spinning.

'Almost there,' Adam's hand twisted the targeting control. 'Can I fire?'

'Yes,' Erimem said sharply. 'Fire now!'

A lance of golden light shot from a laser nest discretely position at the front of the liner, narrowly missing the Drofen ship by a few metres.

'Shit,' Adam hissed. 'Bollocks and arse and shit.'

'Do you ever win any of your games?' Andy asked.

Adam fired again. He was closer but missed by centimetres. 'Shitehawk!' He made another adjustment... the laser lanced out again and the corner of the Drofen ship erupted in a bright explosion.

'I'd still toast you at *Call of Duty*,' Andy said quietly.

Erimem's voice sounded sharply across the flight deck. 'We are not finished yet.'

On screen, small ships were detaching from the ailing Drofen warship and arrowing towards the *Andromedan Princess*. 'Are those escape pods?' she asked.

'No.' They were surprised that it was Tom who answered. 'They're the ships the Drofen used to attack the liner before. They bury their fronts into the hull.'

'We haven't got a hope if they get aboard,' Andy said.

Erimem nodded. 'Fire the deflector again. That should stop...'

Andy had already operated the controls. The seven sharp, snout-like ships were slammed backwards by the deflector wave. They toppled out of control towards the glowing globe of Kestra. Their hulls began to glow as they came into contact with the upper edges of the atmosphere.

'Yes,' Andy said. 'That stopped them. I don't think they've got the power to break free of the gravity.'

'Good,' Erimem said coldly. 'They will be at home with the wild beasts on that planet.'

'They'll be lucky if they don't burn up long before that,' said Andy. 'More's the pity. I'd rather see them get some of their own medicine.'

One of the crew, a young ginger-haired boy spoke from Andy's side. 'There's a message coming in from the *Saint-Saens*. I mean, Captain, there's a...'

Erimem waved a hand to quiet him. 'Let us see it.'

The screen changed, showing the flight deck of the battleship. Captain Watson was bleeding heavily from a cut to his head and looked like he was being held upright by Lee.

'Tell me, which part of "stay out of this" did you not understand?' Watson asked.

The part which involved us abandoning our allies,' Erimem answered. 'I am pleased that you survived.'

'Not everybody did,' Watson said heavily. 'We lost sixty out of two hundred and twenty.'

'That is a heavy loss,' Erimem said, sympathetically. 'That is a burden you will carry.'

Watson agreed. 'Goes with being captain.' Watson changed tack. He was not a man to wallow in his misfortunes. 'Erimem, you know these Drofen better than we do. What would you...'

The screen crackled and split as a third face joined the conversation. It was leathery with a long, extended snout. 'Arumam?' is said, struggling with human words. 'Why has Arumam the prophet turned against us?'

'Prophet?' Watson looked bemused but was quieted as Erimem spoke.

'Why do the Drofen attack the ship of the prophet?'

'Because it was Vallaren's holy word.' The Drofen came a slight movement of obeisance as it used the name "Vallaren".

Erimem saw that Watson had noticed the movement as well. 'Your explanation does not satisfy me,' she said to the Drofen Prime. 'You will come to my ship alone and you will give a full explanation to me in person. 'If I am satisfied, you will be forgiven and allowed to live.' She indicated for the communication for the Drofen to be ended. 'Can you put me on a secure connection to Captain Watson?'

The boy at communications nodded. 'I can scramble you on audio only.'

'Do it.' A moment later she was talking briefly with Watson. 'I will need your marines on board when the Drofen Prime gets here,' Erimem said.

'And I need to decant troops to your ship so we can start repairs,' Watson answered.

'Of course, yes.'

'You'll need to do the hard work in docking,' Watson continued. 'We're in bad shape. We wouldn't have survived much longer.'

'We will be with you in a few minutes,' Erimem said before looking to her communications officer. 'Send a message to the Drofen Prime, one way only. Tell it that we will send a signal when it pleases me to give it an audience. Tell it that it will come to this ship when I send for it and not before. Send exactly that message.'

The boy looked dubious but agreed. 'Yes, ma'am.'

'So,' Andy said, 'you're a prophet now? What's that all about?'

Erimem shook her head. 'I do not have a Shaggy.'

'*Scooby*,' Andy corrected. 'You do not have a *Scooby*.' She nodded over at Adam, who was a keeping watch over the Drofen ship with his laser primed. 'I think you're sorted for the other one.'

CHAPTER NINE

The acrid stench of burning plastic and metal filled the *Saint-Saens*. Captain Watson and his First Officer met Erimem as she emerges through the airlock's hatch.

'We're in much worse shape than I wanted to let on over an open channel,' Watson said simply. 'Simple fact is that she's beyond our ability to repair out here in space. She needs six months in a shipyard to be properly spaceworthy.'

Andy had accompanied Erimem across to the damaged cruiser. 'Can you get her back to dock?'

A weary sigh escaped from Watson. 'We can't escape orbit at the moment. Main engines are damaged beyond repair. They need replaced. All we have is thrusters.' He rubbed a hand across his eyes. 'We still have comms so we have been able to send a message to fleet HQ. It'll take months to tow the ship back to the shipyard, though.'

Erimem indicated the airlock. 'Make whatever use of the liner you have to.'

'Commander Lee already has a thought on that,' Watson said.

'Indeed,' Lee took over. 'Liners of this classification are built in low orbit. There are clamps on the underside for boosters to be attached. They are of a standard size also used in the military. If we could clamp ourselves to your underside, we can use the engineering airlocks to move back and forward between the ships and we could also piggyback the Saint-Saens into your power system. That would let us take our own systems off-line for repairs. We'd be able to make quicker progress that way.'

'Makes sense to me,' Andy said.

'Then you should do it,' Erimem said, 'and I would suggest repairing your weapons first.'

'They are pretty much all that's still working,' Watson said sourly.

'Then we should link the ships as you suggest,' Erimem said briskly, 'and do it quickly. I would very much like to hear what the Drofen Prime has to say.'

A single Drofen attack ship docked with the *Andromedan Princess*. The hatch opened, allowing the Drofen Prime access to the liner. Twelve armed marines formed an arc, their weapons aimed squarely at the Prime as it boarded the ship.

'If you attack anyone or try to breach this cordon you will be killed here,' Erimem said.

'Why does Arumam turn against us?'

'Why do you think you have the right to question a prophet?' she snapped back. 'You are here to answer my question not to ask them.' Erimem raised her chin. 'You will kneel and these men will take you to a place in which I will question your faith.'

'No.'

Erimem stared at the Prime without a hint of fear. 'You defy me, little thing?' She took a confident step closer. 'You are only Prime of the Drofen. I am the prophet. I will make you kneel.'

Two marines fired, slamming tranquiliser darts into the Prime's hide. The Prime staggered and then toppled forward on its face.

'That was impressive,' Watson said quietly. 'Have you been a prophet before?'

Erimem chuckled softly. 'That was easy. Being a living god was much harder.'

Marines ran forward with heavy chains. The Prime's arms and legs were bound tightly. Once it was secured, the Prime was dragged away.

'Why am I in chains?'

The Drofen Prime's voice echoed around the executive gymnasium and it strained against the chains holding it in place.

Solid chains from its ankles, wrists, waist and neck were attached
to bars solidly secured to the walls. Beneath the grey, leathery
skin, its muscles strained but the chains held firm.

'You question the prophet,' Erimem answered. 'You
question me and you attack my ship.'

'Yes.'

Erimem made a point of not looking to any of the others at
the side of the gym. A prophet, like a pharaoh, didn't need to
look to anyone else for advice or support. 'You attacked my ship
and the ship of my soldiers and you have the affront to blame the
loyal Vallaren for this outrage? I should have killed you already.'

'She's very good at this,' Watson murmured to Andy.'

'She's had practice.'

'Why would Vallaren send you to kill a prophet?' Erimem
demanded.

'I do not question Vallaren.'

'No matter what you claim he orders you to do?'

'Vallaren's instructions are clear,' Prime said. 'We must
absolve all of creation.'

'And how will you do that?' Erimem asked.

'Why do you not know?'

'I do not doubt myself,' Erimem snapped. 'It is your faith
being put to the test and you have given me many reasons to
doubt you. So tell me how you will absolve all of creation. *Tell
me!*'

'In fire, as Vallaren commands... as *you* command.'

Every eye focused on Erimem. She ignored the scrutiny.
'How did I order it?' she asked. 'How well do you know your
faith? How loyal are you to what you have been taught?'

'I devote my life to purifying creation.'

'And yet you are unable to tell me how,' Erimem said
harshly. 'You are only words. You are of no worth. You betray
your faith.'

'We purify in fire,' the Prime snarled. 'We will burn all of
creation.'

'Why? Because Vallaren told you to do it?'

The Prime's head tilted. 'Because *you* told Vallaren to do it.'

Erimem struggled not to let her surprise show. Her time at
court had given her practice at playing political games and

wearing what Andy called a "poker face". 'At least you know something,' she said acidly, 'but do you know when I said this to Vallaren?'

'A thousand years ago.'

Erimem nodded approvingly. 'I have aged well in a thousand years.'

The door opened and Lee entered. The effect on the Prime was instant and violent. It shook at its chains with all its might, desperately trying to get to Lee. 'That is an abomination. It is an offence against creation.'

'Actually, it is my friend,' Erimem said, bobbing her head towards the door and leading her group out. She didn't wait for Lee to report to Watson. 'What did you find from the Drofen's shuttle?' she asked the First Officer.

'A link to their ship's computer,' Lee answered. 'We downloaded everything we could and put it through the translator.

'And?' Watson pressed.

'There are hundreds of ships,' Lee answered, 'all of them based on a planet in the Permilon system. The charts call in Bermal.'

'You said the ships were based on this world,' Erimem said. 'Does that mean they are not there now?'

Lee shook her head. 'They have been sent to attack planets, colonies and space stations. It was these Drofen who destroyed Venulatu and the other worlds.'

'Because they're religious nut-jobs,' Andy said. 'I'm cool with religion but not with loonies who abuse it. Who'd have thought the Drofen would get God?'

Watson's gaze was on Erimem. 'They also seem to have got *you*,' he said warily.

'For something you did a thousand years ago,' Andy added.

'Which is obviously impossible,' Watson said, rubbing his chin in thought. 'Could the names just be a coincidence? That thing did say "Arumam" rather than Erimem?'

'How many people do you know by either name?' Erimem asked.

'One,' Watson admitted.

Erimem nodded. 'Then we can assume that it is not a

coincidence.'

Watson nodded to himself. 'We'll think on that. Meantime, we have to get a warning back to headquarters about these Drofen ships about to attack who knows where.' He looked at Lee quickly. 'Except you've already told them, haven't you?'

Lee nodded. 'I assumed that you would want that message sent as soon as possible.'

'You assumed right.'

Lee took no pleasure in the praise. 'Our ships are no match for theirs in a one on one fight and they outnumber us. With respect to Erimem, we only survived this encounter because she took them by surprise.'

'We have to put up a defence of some sort,' Watson objected, 'if only to let civilians escape.'

'No,' Erimem said. 'Direct your ships to this planet of theirs...' She looked to Lee for the name.

'Bermal.'

'Yes, Bermal. Direct all of your ships there. Get them within range of Bermal before the Drofen attack, then announce that you will be launching an attack on Bermal. The Drofen will turn back.'

'Are you sure?' Andy asked. 'They've gone *Blues Brothers*. They're on a mission from God.'

'They will turn back to protect this Vallaren,' Erimem said, 'especially if they think the prophet Arumam is there to kill him.'

'And why would they think that?' Andy asked.

'Because we will tell them that she is,' Erimem said coldly, 'and because if the attacks are not halted it will probably be true.'

Helena was the loudest dissenting voice against Erimem's plan. 'I've got civilians on board this ship,' she said angrily. 'Do you really think we should take them back into a war zone?'

'No,' Erimem answered sadly, 'but if we do not do this, billions will die.'

'I still don't like it,' Helena said.

An hour after sending a hyperlink communication to Headquarters with the plan to attack Nermal, a reply came that the fleet was *en route*. The *Andromedan Princess* was more than powerful enough to reach her top speed with the *Saint-Saens* still attached. The Drofen ship tried to move to intercept as the Earth ships pulled away. It managed a single weak shot but that shot sealed its fated. Captain Watson instructed his gunners to target the injured Drofen ship. An instant later it flared as bright as a sun and then was gone, reduced to debris.

The action had surprised both Tom and Adam. Erimem knew that Andy and Ibrahim hadn't liked the brutality of the response but they accepted it as part of war. Tom was still shaken by the violence around them but refused the chance to return home. As for Adam... she wasn't sure what he was thinking. If she had to guess she'd say that he was weighing his part in the death of so many Drofen. He had been the one who destroy their engines. He was weighing the justice of the act.

A yawn overtook Erimem and she realised how tired she was. It had been a long day. 'How long until we meet the fleet?' she asked Andy.

'Sixteen hours at current speed,' Haniya answered, and then she looked mortified as she realised the question hadn't been aimed at her. 'Oh. Sorry.'

Andy waved away any hint of offence. 'Saved me answering.'

Erimem spoke quietly to Watson. 'Captain, I suggest as many of the crew as possible get some rest. Today has been a long day and tomorrow will be the same.'

Watson agreed and set a minimum of six hours of bunk-time for every member of the crew.

An hour later, Erimem was back in the bedroom of the suite she shared with Adam. She showered before bed but it didn't shake her exhaustion. In the bathroom mirror she noticed that her hair was getting long. It was past her shoulders. There were times she hankered for the simpler times when it would all just be shaved off regularly. She wasn't sure she would suit being bald anymore, but it would certainly make drying herself after a shower quicker. She pulled on her pyjamas and climbed carefully into bed so that she wouldn't wake Adam. Already he seemed to be asleep. She had just turned the small light out when he spoke.

'Is it always like this?'

Erimem thought before answering. 'Not exactly,' she said. 'Sometimes it is just silly fun with friends. But sometimes people need help.'

'Even if it means going to war?'

'I am a warrior,' she answered simply. 'I led Egypt's armies in battle many times.'

'Okay.'

And that was that. A few minutes later, they were both asleep.

The *Andromedan Princess* joined the Earth fleet exactly on time, slowing its pace to match the speed of the twenty strong convoy. More ships joined the fleet by the hour and there were over sixty battleships in the flotilla when the broadcast was made that Arumam was returning to confront Vallaren on Bermal. At that point the Earth fleet put up a jamming signal stopping the Drofen ships from contacting Vallaren.

In his citadel on the planet, Vallaren had heard the signal Erimem had sent. He should have been afraid or at least concerned. Instead, his heart burst with joy. Arumam was coming back to him. After all the centuries, he would see her again. Everything he had done was vindicated in that single moment. She was coming back to see the great works he had done. She was coming back to praise him.

She was coming back for the end of the universe.

The Earth fleet dropped under light speed half a million kilometres from Bermal. The *Andromedan Princess* had been designated a hospital ship and ordered to remain towards the rear of the fleet.

Admiral Cartwright, in command of the fleet, was not a man of great imagination. He had his rule book and he liked to stick to it. Whatever the civilians aboard the *Andromedan Princess* had done – and he paid little attention when Captain Watson gave him details of the action – this was a military matter, and the coincidence of this twenty-something woman sharing a name with a prophet, that was something that could be investigated later if anyone thought it was worth following up.

Erimem had taken an immediate dislike to Cartwright.

It was clear that Captain Watson didn't like Cartwright much either, and that the feeling was mutual. On the flight deck of the *Andromedan Princess*, Watson and Erimem watched the first engagement of the Earth ships and the Drofen ship defending the planet. The Earth fleet outnumbered the defensive forces but the Drofen fought ferociously. Though clearly limited in his thinking, Cartwright was resolute and had prepared for the engagement. The first wave of sixteen Earth ships engaged the Drofen ship, like sets of heavyweight boxers swinging hard to land knockout blows. Cartwright pressed an advantage by ordering larger ships which had been held back to bombard the Drofen craft with heavy missiles. The barrage found its mark more often than it missed, causing crippling damage to the Drofen vessels, but as the red ships failed, they launched their attack ships towards the Earth fleet. The third wave of Cartwright's plan fell into place as the two great fighter carriers in the fleet launched their squadrons. The small, nimble fighters made quick work of the Drofen's breaching ships, blasting them apart spilling the carcasses of the dead Drofen into space.

Admiral Cartwright's flagship hailed the planet. 'Vallaren, this is Admiral Cartwright. You will surrender yourself to us at once.'

'Where is Arumam?' was the only reply.

Cartwright did not possess an abundance of patience. 'I am in command here, not some girl.'

'Is Arumam your prisoner?'

'Your Arumam is irrelevant,' Cartwright said.

'Not to us.'

A hundred Drofen warships blinked into existence in orbit over the planet. They opened fire within seconds. The Earth fleet fought back ferociously, hitting the Drofen ships with all of the weapons in their armoury. The Earth fighters swarmed their enemy but were picked off as easily as if they were flies being swatted away.

The battle was watched from the flight deck of the *Andromedan Princess*.

'We are going to lose,' Erimem said flatly.

Watson agreed. 'You're right. Cartwright should have checked there were no other ships in the system. He was warned.'

On screen a Drofen ship flared and exploded.

'However, this does give us a chance to reach the surface,' Erimem said. 'I need one of your shuttles.'

'We were ordered to stay here,' Watson answered.

Erimem shrugged. 'I am not in your fleet. I do not take orders.'

'But you do want to take one of my shuttles.'

'And one of your pilots. I cannot fly your ships.'

Watson sighed. 'You don't ask for much, do you?'

The shuttle weaved through the chaos of the battle, avoiding the larger shots with ease and steering clear of the smaller ship. The planet was approximately Earth size with similar gravity. It was dry, though, an arid planet on which water was a precious resource. That meant there were few clouds in the sky.

Inside the small ship, Erimem had managed to set aside her anger. She had wanted a single pilot to take her to the planet's surface and then leave her to find and face this Vallaren. It made sense for her to face him alone. He would talk to her if he thought she was a prophet, and if thing went badly wrong she could use her travel ring to return to her Habitat. Captain Watson had refused to countenance her going alone, and so had her friends. That was why she arrived on the surface outside of the citadel with Andy and an escort of two marines. Adam had wanted to go with them but Erimem had refused to let him take the risk. They had parted in anger.

'You should have let me come alone,' Erimem said to Andy.

'Should have, would have, could have... didn't.'

The planet was dry and arid with a constant wind blowing sand in gusts across open dusty plains. The Citadel was carved into a mountain. The strange, star-like cross symbol the Drofen had daubed on the walls of the ship was carved above what was obviously the entrance to the citadel. Large, carved pillars stood on either side of the wide opening. Drofen moved in other openings on other parts of the mountain. They had dug some kind of shelter from the stone.

Drofen moved towards Erimem's party, a mixture of hate, curiosity, hunger and what may have been awe on their faces. Their attention was focused on Erimem and again she knew that she should have come alone, but there was nothing she could do about that now. She had told Andy and the two marines to stay close by her side. Drofen were approaching them, lining the path leading to the Citadel.

The marines' hands twitched nervously on their weapons.

'Be calm,' Erimem said. 'They will not kill the prophet. Not yet, anyway.'

'You hope.' Andy moved a little closer to Erimem. So did the marines.

The interior of the Citadel was carved deep into the stone of the mountain. The star symbol was carved into the walls at regular intervals and Drofen stood in every roughly hewn arch to keep the party moving along the course chosen for then.

'They should get *Changing Rooms* or something in to fix the decor.' Andy tried to inject some levity but it sounded hollow.

'Arumam!'

A man stood in a wide corridor in front of wide metal doors. Above the arch was that same sun/cross symbol.

The voice was undeniably Vallaren. 'Arumam. You have come back.'

'Have I?' Erimem asked warily.

Vallaren ignored the doubts in her voice. 'Now I know we will be successful.'

'Do you?'

Vallaren pushed the doors open. 'Oh, yes.'

Beyond the door, at the heart of the great chamber, a miniature star-like shape glowed. The moment Erimem and Andy stepped through the doorway, the shape flared violently, pulsing outward like a heart beating.

Screaming pain shot through both Erimem and Andy, and they clutched each other to stay upright.

The star pulsed again.

This time the pain was worse. Andy couldn't stop herself from screaming.

Vallaren just smiled more broadly.

CHAPTER TEN

It took Andy a long moment to realise the source of the pain tearing through her body. The time travel ring she wore on her finger screamed up her arm, searing its way through her nerves to her brain. She staggered back, out of the room and felt her senses return. She didn't realise for a moment that it was Erimem who had dragged her back outside. The Egyptian looked as bad as Andy felt.

'Ring?' Andy hissed to Erimem.

Her friend nodded, plucked the time travel ring from her finger and pushed it into her pocket. Andy quickly did the same, ignoring the pain that always came with separation from a travel ring.

After a deep breath, Erimem stepped into the chamber. The star maintained its luminosity, pulsing rhythmically. Andy followed. She could feel a heat building in her pocket from the ring but at least there was no pain.

'I knew you would come back,' Vallaren said. 'One day, before the end, you would come back.'

'How did you know?' Erimem asked.

'I had faith.'

Andy caught Erimem's eye. They knew each other well enough for Erimem to stay quiet and let Andy take over. 'When did you meet Arumam?' she asked Vallaren. I have asked her many times but she will not tell me.'

Erimem played along. 'We are here now, my loyal slave. Perhaps you have earned the right to hear.'

'Tell me please.'

'I...' Erimem stopped, apparently toying with her slave. She turned to Vallaren. 'Should I tell her, Vallaren?'

'It is a tale I tell our brothers,' Vallaren said. 'Let her hear it.'

'*You* tell her,' Erimem suggested. 'Tell her as if she was one of our noble brothers seeking to bring purification and absolution.'

You crafty bitch, thought Andy. *Hiding that you know bugger all behind swagger and a few overheard words.*

'Please tell me,' Andy wheedled. 'The prophet teases me.'

Vallaren spoke, as if the words had been spoken so often they were a prayer.

'Once, long ago, this world was home to a monastery. The Monks of Varule were known for their wisdom and kindness. Their every thought was for the physical and spiritual betterment of their fellow creatures. In one man, there was a fervour to help every creature he could. He was young and modest but his gifts were extraordinary. He had been blessed with a faith that marked him from youth as a potential abbot. His ability to empathise with others and to form bonds with them was only matched by his prowess as a scientist. The depth and breadth of his knowledge was quite stunning. From evolutionary biology to chemistry to sub-particle astrophysics, there had never been a mind quite the same. The Great Godhead worshipped by the Monks of Varule also thought this monk extraordinary – indeed He had made the monk so special and precious – and one great day He showed His favour by sending a great visitation to the monk, and that visitation was the prophet Arumam. She came with her servant in a storm of fire, and there she gave the monk his epiphany, his mission. He was to find his soldiers and to bring the peace and justice of the Godhead through fire. The monk knew what had to be done and he was given eternal life to achieve his holy mission. He thanked the Great Godhead and devoted himself to that mission.'

Vallaren stopped his speech. It had been delivered word-perfect without a hesitation. It was a story he had told many times before. He expected Erimem and Andy to be impressed. They disappointed him.

'Pop culture reference,' Andy said. 'David Koresh or Charles Manson.'

Realisation spread across Erimem's face and she nodded slowly. 'The film we saw on your Netflix. I read more on similar men later for a dissertation.' She nodded. 'I think you are correct.' She focused her attention on Vallaren. 'You have told that story many times but how much do you remember of my visitation?'

'Your *divine* visitation,' Andy corrected.

'Tell me how you remember me,' Erimem said to Vallaren. Andy recognised the tone. She had heard it enough in the university, girls reeling their boys in, manipulating them. Erimem was far more capable with it than Andy had expected. Maybe it was similar to how she had dealt with the priests and politicians in Egypt.

Vallaren was too rapt by the thought of the prophet's return to be concerned by her tone. 'You were dressed then just as you are now.'

'Really?'

'Yes,' Vallaren nodded vigorously.

'What else?' Erimem coaxed.

'You held in your hand the ring you wore when you came in today.'

Erimem plucked the ring from her pocket. It began to burn as it came into contact with her skin. 'This ring?'

'Yes,' Vallaren answered. 'Don't you remember?'

'It is your memory that concerns me,' Erimem deflected. 'Do you remember what you were doing when we met?'

'Working on a matter transportation device,' Vallaren replied. 'It could have eliminated poverty in the universe.'

'Instead, you now choose to eliminate the universe?' Erimem said.

'As you instructed me,' Vallaren said. He had begun to look confused. 'Are you truly the prophet?'

Erimem didn't answer directly. 'Many things requires answers,' she said. She took two steps towards the pulsing star. As she closed the pulses grew larger and more violent. Within a few seconds, the star had engulfed them all.

Andy swore loudly and swore a lot. She was inside something similar to the storm of energy created by the travel rings when they moved through space and time, only this was more violent and utterly wild, lacking the structure she was used to.

Images of times and places, people and events she had never known swept by. Images, sounds, sensations. Other people's experiences, other species' experiences.

They were in a laboratory.

No, they weren't *in* it. They were observing it. Shit, that wasn't right either. Somehow they were there but not there at the same time. It was disconcerting and made her want to throw up.

Erimem looked to be in worse shape than Andy felt. Then again, Erimem was still clutching her travel ring. Either the pain was fading or Erimem was coming to terms with it. Her eyes opened and she looked ahead, forcing herself to focus.

'Where is this?' Erimem said.

It was Vallaren who answered. 'It is my laboratory. Over a thousand years ago, it is my laboratory.'

The familiar figure of Vallaren was also in the laboratory, picking himself up from the floor.

'Can he see us?' Erimem asked.

The Vallaren in the laboratory answered. 'I hear you. Who are you?'

'This is it,' the other Vallaren, the one inside the time storm with them, said. 'This is the visitation from the prophet Arumam.'

'Prophet?' the younger Vallaren picked up on the word. 'I am blessed to be visited by a prophet.' He dropped to his knees. 'I am not worthy to be in your presence.'

'I remember this,' the older Vallaren said in wonder. 'A hand reached from the vision and helped me rise.' Almost as if hypnotised, he extended his hand towards his younger self. 'I remember the words... I remember the voice... my voice. Rise and stand,' he said boldly.

Both Erimem and Andy reached for Vallaren to stop him from making physical contact with his younger self but moving within the electrical storm was sluggish. They were too slow.

The two Vallarens touched fingertips as if recreating Michelangelo's art.

The electrical storm erupted in a huge explosion of energy.

Far in the past, Vallaren winced in pain but opened his eyes. As his eyes opened, so did his mind. Thoughts, experiences, images, languages, knowledge... an avalanche of things he could not know threatened to overwhelm his mind, but he held firm under the onslaught, assimilating the information, somehow recognising it all as being his.

He *understood*.

The prophet had come and given him this great knowledge, and with that knowledge he had been given a mission. He knew exactly what was wanted of him.

'Are you all right, Brother Vallaren?'

One of the older monks had run in and knelt beside him. Vallaren hadn't seen Eckon enter the ruined lab.

Picking up a broken shard of glass, Vallaren slashed across Eckon's throat.

He had released Eckon. He had saved him.

Vallaren had begun his holy mission.

Andy landed hard on the stone floor of the Citadel. Her pained was doubled when she acted as a landing mat for Erimem.

Vallaren landed a few metres away. He was winded but rapt.

Erimem scrabbled across the stone floor and picked up her time travel ring, which she had dropped as she landed.

Andy knew Erimem would be asking questions soon enough. She had to come up with a theory on what had happened. As it happened, the facts were forming an idea quickly.

'What happened?' Erimem demanded. She was wincing with pain as she held the ring, but she was ignoring it.

'I'm not sure,' Andy answered, 'but if he was working on matter transportation, I have a question. Hey, Vallaren,' she called, 'when you did your matter transportation experiments, did you give any consideration to how manipulating space would affect time locally?'

'No,' Vallaren answered. 'We had no wish to manipulate time.'

'It's called space-time for a reason,' Andy snapped. 'You can't affect one without affecting the other.' She looked to

Erimem. 'He caused some damage to time in the past which attracted us in the present – or future if we're being pernickity – but that attracted us...'

'Which made us affect him and set him on his quest, which brought us here...'

Andy nodded. 'And sent us back to make him start his quest. We're the cause and the effect.'

'I hate time travel,' Erimem muttered.

'Somehow the time distortion affected him,' Andy added. 'It's extended his life.'

'Long enough to fulfil his own prophecy,' Erimem agreed.

Vallaren was lost in his own thoughts. New memories seemed to have been freed. 'All of these years I thought Arumam was the prophet. I was wrong.'

'We could have told you that,' Andy grumbled.

Vallaren ignored her. '*She* did not give the prophecy. *I* did.' His brow furrowed. 'But the Godhead did not tell me what to say. I only shared with myself.' His head tilted and his eyes widened in some semblance of manic understanding. 'If the words were mine and I gave the Godhead's words, then I must be the Godhead. *I am the living Godhead.*'

'He thinks he's God,' Andy muttered. 'The energy released by meeting himself must have fried his last bit of brain.'

Erimem snorted dismissively. 'There is only one living god here, and that is me.'

'And you resigned from the job,' Andy added.

There had never been a great deal of hope of persuading Vallaren he was wrong. His eyes showed they had no chance of dissuading him of the idea that he was a god.

'You are not prophets. You are not sent by the Godhead. You are heretics.'

Erimem punched Vallaren hard in the face. He dropped back to the floor and she kicked him into unconsciousness before he could move.

'Guessing the plan is to get the hell out of here?' Andy said.

'As fast as we can,' Erimem agreed.

They left the Inner Sanctum, bowing obsequiously and giving thanks to Vallaren, giving the impression that he was at prayer. They walked quickly but calmly back towards the shuttle.

The screech of the Drofen told them that their deception had been uncovered and they ran the last few metres, closing the hatch just before the first of the Drofen reached the shuttle.

The small ship blasted off before they could buckle their seatbelts. They didn't care. They had escaped from the surface.

Unfortunately, what was waiting in space was far worse.

Drofen ships had broken away from the battle with the fleet from Earth to bring their weapons towards the shuttle. The pilot weaved and ducked the shuttle, moving it through the Drofen sleet with speed. Three Drofen ships were hit by friendly fire before the heavy weapons were quieted.

Andy had taken the co-pilot's chair more by accident than intention. '*Saint-Saens*, this is the shuttle. We're coming in hot as hell.'

Captain Watson's voice answered tersely, 'We're busy just now. Whatever you did down there has really annoyed them.'

'We discovered the truth,' Erimem shouted.

'And it sucks,' Andy added.

'We're under attack,' Watson replied. The Drofen are trying to breach the liner's shields.'

'We will be there in a few minutes,' Erimem said.

'If we're lucky,' Andy muttered.

The shuttle entered the Saint-Saens' shuttle bay a few minutes later. By the time Erimem and Andy had reached the *Andromedan Princess*' flight deck, there was already a running battle on the liner.

'They breached in one place,' Watson said. 'We're holding them but it's no better than stalemate.'

'Why aren't they just overrunning the ship?' Andy asked.

'Because we have their leader,' Erimem replied. 'They fear we will kill it if our situation is desperate.'

'That buys us a bit of time, I suppose,' Watson said.

'No,' Erimem said sharply, 'it gives us an advantage.'

The Drofen Prime roared with a rage sharpened by millennia of evolution. He was the ultimate hunter and now he was held in chains by what he saw as no more than meat.

One of his captors smelled wrong. It moved wrong. He could smell the familiar scent of the others, hear their heartbeat, taste them in his mind. This one was different. It was unnatural, an abomination.

Still in chains, the Prime had been placed into a cage. The mesh on the cage was too fine to even push its talons through. It was being moved through the corridors of the human ship.

Why was it being moved?

What were they going to do with it?

If their plan was murder, then the Prime would face that with the courage of its faith, and tear as many of them from this world as he could.

An alarm sounded in the corridor. The humans began to make panicking sounds and ran back from where they had come. The Prime understood their fear. He could sense his brothers coming. He could hear them, smell them.

And then he saw his brothers, dozens of them. They swarmed the cage, shattering it and setting him free.

The Prime screeched and the exulted as the rest of its horde chorused with him. They would swarm this ship and devour the humans. They began to swarm outwards along the corridor in both directions... and in both directions they found that the emergency bulkheads had slid into position, sealing them into a small section of corridor.

The Prime screeched and the Horde responded by clawing at the doors and walls, searching for an escape.

Somewhere in the screeching, the Prime heard a human voice.

'Stop your attempts to escape,' it said in that weak, human way. 'The corridor in which you are trapped is open to space. The atmosphere is only held in place by a force field. If you continue trying to escape, we will switch off the force-field and vent you into space.'

The human words worked through the Prime's brain. It understood what the human had said and it remembered seeing the hole out into space with the glow of the energy barrier beyond... but it couldn't deny its nature. The Drofen couldn't deny their nature. They had been called to swarm by their Prime and that had released a hormone sending them all into a frenzied bloodlust. Even the Prime couldn't resist that primal urge. It threw itself at the safety door.

Captain Watson's finger hovered over the control which would kill the force-field in the section of corridor where the Drofen were trapped. He had no qualms about killing in battle but this felt dangerously close to murder. He had gratefully accepted Erimem's plan to trap the Drofen but he hadn't actually thought he might have to coldly eject them into space.

'It is their nature to fight,' Erimem said.

Commander Lee looked up from her console. 'It is possible that they might break through the emergency doors. They have already been put through stress by one sudden depressurisation.'

Watson's finger moved closer to the control.

'Perhaps I should do this,' Lee offered. 'I am more acquainted with this ship's systems.'

There was nothing Watson would have appreciated more than agreeing to that, and his respect and affection for his First Officer grew. 'I'm captain,' he said quietly. 'This down to me.'

A female hand pushed Watson's aside and pressed down on the control.

On the view-screen, the Drofen were dragged through the air and expelled through the small opening in the hull as the forcefield was deactivated. Their arms and legs thrashed and their flesh was caught on the ragged edge of the hole, leaving strips of skin attached to the metal as the bodies were forced through the hole in a flailing mass by the escaping air. Within seconds it was all over. The corridor was empty.

Captain Lescal gently pressed the button to restore the force-field and atmosphere in the corridor. 'I'm a captain, too. Better that I did it.'

Watson eyed the army captain dubiously. 'Perhaps you had more right than me.'

Lescal nodded. 'I did.'

'Where is your nephew?' Watson asked, eager to turn his thoughts away from the killing of the Drofen.

'Fed and asleep in the sickbay, under the eye of that civilian doctor,' Lescal answered.

The liner shook violently as a shot hit its shields.

It was Erimem who spoke up. 'I think the Drofen know what we did to their Prime.'

'Can we outrun them?' Watson asked.

Lee answered without taking her gaze from the screen. 'No. They are zero point one-four faster than our top speed.'

'You should not run away,' Erimem said.

Watson turned to the young woman is bemusement. 'What do you suggest we use to fight? Those pocket lasers used for asteroids?'

Erimem pointed at the planet ahead. 'I suggest we go straight ahead at that. Use the ship to destroy the Citadel.'

'Three more of our fleet are disabled,' Lee called. 'Admiral Cartwright is reported as... incapacitated.' She nodded.

Watson knew that the eyes of the room – probably the fleet – were on him. He didn't have time to delay. 'All right. What's the plan? I'm not comfortable with crashing somebody else's ship into a planet.'

'That is good,' Erimem said, 'because I did not mean this ship.'

'What?'

'The *Saint-Saens*,' Andy said. 'We can't transfer everybody to her – she's too badly damaged to be space-worthy.'

'But she would make a perfect bomb,' Erimem interjected, 'if the engines were overloading with...' she looked to Andy. 'It's your plan. You explain.'

'Anti-matter,' Andy nodded. 'You've got anti-matter in your engines. Engines which are, to use the technical term, absolutely buggered. Crash the ship into Vallaren's Citadel. It'll blow the place up.'

'It could blow half the planet up,' Watson answered. 'I can't destroy my ship.'

The *Andromedan Princess* shook as another barrage hit the shields.

Lee reported efficiently, 'The ship's shielding will not last long, captain. A destroyer just took heavy damage by shielding us.'

'The plan is to blow up a big chunk of the planet,' Andy said quickly. 'The Drofen will follow any ship that's attacking the surface. If they're close enough, the explosion will take enough of them out to even things up.'

'I understand that you have a responsibility to your ship,' Erimem said quickly, 'but it is better for you to destroy it in winning the battle than in the Drofen destroying it and unleashing Vallaren's madness on the universe.'

Watson frowned. 'When you say madness...'

'He's completely Wanstead Park,' Andy said. 'That's two stages beyond Barking.'

Watson's frown deepened and Erimem explained. 'Andy is trying to say that Vallaren is insane and we saw what had caused his insanity.'

'Too long a story to share here,' Andy said quickly.

Lee's voice came from her station. 'Two more of our fleet have been incapacitated.'

That made up Watson's mind. 'Do it. Lee, it'll need your command codes to power the engines to critical. You go with them.'

'Yes, sir.'

Watson caught Lee's arm. 'And record it in the log that destroying the *Saint-Saens* is *my* decision. If anyone is carrying the can for that, it should be me.'

'As you wish.'

Lee led the way off of the Flight Deck at a run, with Erimem and Andy close behind.

'All right,' Watson said, 'contact the fleet and tell them what we're doing – and put it on an open channel so those monsters can hear us. And, navigation... take us in.'

Andy was fast on her feet. She had been on the athletics team at school, at least until the Boob Fairy had paid her a visit and she had become too self-conscious to run. She was still quick, though, and Erimem was annoyingly fleet of foot, but they both struggled to keep up with Lee. On a flat, even surface her android physique was easily faster than either of them.

They dropped into the warship, passing the last few remaining evacuating members of the repair crew. In the corridors, wall panels had been stripped from walls baring wires and conduits. The Saint-Saens' flight deck was in equal disrepair.

Lieutenant Commander Lee input her command codes and started the ship's engines on a countdown to detonation.

Andy, however was troubled by the readings. 'It's not enough.' she said softly.

'What do you mean?' Erimem asked.

Andy tapped at the display. We'll explode and blow up Vallaren's temple place but we won't blow the planet or much of their fleet.'

Adam Docherty was seething.

He had contacted the flight deck to find out what had happened to Erimem and Andy only to be dismissively told by a junior officer that she had gone to the *Saint-Saens*.

'They want us to stay here,' Adam said sourly.

Ibrahim sniffed. 'And you say?'

'I say baws tae that,' Adam growled, letting his accent thicken. 'If there's something happening we should be with them.'

'I agree,' Olivia said.

Tom surprised everyone by agreeing. 'So do I.'

'I'm going nowhere,' Helena said. She pointed out of the little office into the sickbay where injured civilians and soldiers filled rows of beds. 'I have patients.' She peered at the sleeping form of baby Alex. 'This one's my favourite.'

'I also like the baby,' Olivia said, 'but I agree with Adam. She should...' her voice stopped as the undeniable sound of an animal breathing and walking stopped nearby.

'There's a Drofen still aboard,' Adam hissed.

Instinctively Tom raised the weapon he had been issued before going to the planet surface. Olivia did the same.

Ibrahim headed for the door. 'We'll protect the sickbay,' Ibrahim promised Helena. 'Nothing will get past us.'

'Just make sure you come back in one piece,' she answered. 'That goes for all of you.'

Carrying their weapons, the four moved to the door of the

sickbay where a single marine looked incredibly nervous. The five set up positions, watching both ways long the corridor. The empty corridor gave an odd, echoing sound to snarls and growls. Eventually, it came into view, moving cautiously towards them. The marine raised his weapon to fire but was halted by Ibrahim.

'Not yet,' he said softly. 'It's too far away to start firing. It moves so fast your sights be playing catch up with it.'

The Drofen moved on muscular, sinewy legs, preparing itself to attack.

'We have two problems,' Andy said. 'One, the explosion won't be big enough and two, the ship will need someone aboard almost to the end to make sure the emergency safeties don't cut in.'

'The latter will be my job,' Lee said. 'Increasing power will be up to you.'

Andy held up her travel ring. Erimem was doing exactly the same at the same time. Andy spoke first. 'These reacted to the energy storm down there. Something tells me adding one of them to the anti-matter reaction would close things down there permanently and make the explosion huge.'

Erimem's head tilted curiously. 'I had exactly the same thought.' She snorted. 'My grandfather put these thoughts in our minds.'

Andy was horrified by the idea. 'He's been in my head? Well, he can piss off with that. He's not my grandad,' she said angrily. 'He can sod off.'

'I will tell him to sod off later,' Erimem promised. 'For now, we should put one of the rings into this anti-matter.'

Andy nodded. 'Okay.' She pressed a button on the panel. 'Bollocks. Communications to the liner are down.' She smiled winningly at Lee. 'Speedy, could you be a love and run one of your hand sets up to somebody on the liner so we can use them to work out our timings?'

'Very well.' Lee ran from the room. After a moment Andy and Erimem followed.

'You disabled the communications,' Erimem said. There was no accusation in her statement. 'You wish to save her life.'

Andy smiled self-consciously. 'Better than having her commit suicide. I turned the communications on again before we left. We can switch off the cut-outs then leave a few seconds before the crash.'

Erimem smiled proudly at her friend. 'You are very sneaky for a good person.' She handed her travel ring to Andy. 'Use this to set the explosion. I will lock the hatch to the liner.'

The Drofen made its move. Shots flew across the corridor but the creature moved with a terrifying, strangely animalistic balletic grace as it avoided the shots. It was only metres away when a shot from Olivia caught its hip. The beast landed awkwardly and still managed to throw itself forward, but much of its forward momentum had been lost. It still carried enough force to knock the marine backwards into Tom. Both staggered and fell to the ground. Ibrahim managed to hit it with two solid blasts from near point blank range, and yet the maddened beast only screamed in pain and continued its attack. A swat from its hand sent Ibrahim reeling, but it howled as Adam and Olivia both slammed shots into its chest. They could smell the burning flesh but the Drofen remained alive and dangerous. Its arm swung back to slash its claws down as Adam.

The Drofen's head erupted in a mass of bone and tissue and brain.

'Go for the head,' Captain Lescal said, holstering her sidearm. 'The bodies seem to have been given some kind of genetic reinforcement.' She helped Ibrahim to his feet. She saw his eyes widen and heard the yells.

Lescal's knees buckled as claws slashed across her back, tearing through her uniform and gouging the skin.

'There's another one.' Adam fired first.

Olivia also opened fire as did Tom and the marine, but somehow the Drofen they hadn't seen managed to lash out with arms and legs striking at several of them at the same time.

Abruptly, the Drofen stopped striking out and began to flail. It was lifted from the ground by Commander Lee. She had one arm wrapped around the beast and another at the back of its neck. Adam raised his weapon to follow Lescal's instruction and fire at the head, but the fight had already ended. With a surge of strength, Lee had ripped the Drofen's head from its neck. She dropped the severed head and the body and then seemed to be aware for the first time that the animal's huge claws had slashed through her uniform, opening her arm deeply. Synthetic blood poured from the wounds.

Sure that there were no more Drofen in the corridor, Ibrahim had the two injured officers carried inside the sickbay.

Helena was relieved to see her friends unharmed but winced at the injuries inflicted on Lee and Lescal.

'Tend to Captain Lescal first,' Lee said.

Helena inspected the first officer's arm quickly. 'I'm the doctor around here. That's my decision. You get treated first if you need it more.' She moved to the bed on which Lescal had been placed face down. One look at the woman's back showed that Lee had been correct. 'Yeah, this is worse.' She pressganged her friends into service. 'Ibrahim, you and Tom try to stop Lee's bleeding. I'm pretty sure she can tell you what coagulant to use. Olivia, you help me get Lescal out of her fatigues.'

Lee struggled against the attention. She held out a radio to Adam. 'Take this to the flight deck. Communications between the ships are down. This is the only way to communicate with the Saint-Saens.'

A knowing look passed between Helena and Ibrahim, who punched an intercom button on the wall. '*Andromedan Princess* sickbay calling *Saint-Saens*.'

Andy's voice crackled. 'Hi. How are you all doing?'

'Better than you'll be when Lee gets her hands on you.'

'It made sense,' Andy answered unapologetically. 'Erimem's just locking things down then we'll be ready to be on our way.'

'So there's no need to take that radio anywhere,' Helena said, turning to where Adam had been.

But Adam had gone.

Erimem was not as quick with computer systems as Andy. There was no surprise about that. Computers were something she dealt with every day but she had not grown up among them and so she still had to pause and take stock occasionally. It was one of those short pauses for thought which allowed Adam Docherty to burst into the *Saint-Saens* just as the hatches began to close.

'You idiot!' Erimem shouted. 'What are you doing here?'

'I'm glad to see you too,' he answered.

The irritation was fading from Erimem's face. 'We just got rid of Lee.'

'Just as well you did. She saved our necks. She looks to be in a bad way though.'

Concern appeared on Erimem's face. 'That is unfortunate.' She sighed, accepting the situation as it now was. 'Tell me what happened on the way to the flight deck.'

Andy was very impressed by her own handiwork. She had the engines ready to detonate, and Erimem's travel ring had been partially twisted so that the energy used to travel was ready to be unleashed. Flashes and crackles of energy began to spark from the ring to the anti-matter containment banks. The electricity flashed like lightning, growing and beginning to fill the engine room.

'Shit! Shit! Shitshitshit!' Looking at the electricity around her, Andy realised it was time to run.

She bolted from the engine room and sprinted through the corridors. She arrived on the flight deck and was surprised to see Erimem was not alone.

'The idea was to get rid of people, not grab your boyfriend.' She waved a hand to quiet their protests. 'Save the lame crap till later. The engine's on its way to exploding.' On cue, the ship was shaken by an impact from a Drofen weapon. 'And they're still pissed at us.'

Captain Watson turned off the communication and looked to his navigation panel. One of the junior officers was there. What was her name? He had read her file. She was from a good service family in Pakistan and on her first voyage... Haniya, that was it. He considered replacing her with a more experienced officer, but she had been on the flight deck here during the last encounter and had acquitted herself admirably according to Erimem.

'Maximum speed, Haniya,' he said. 'You know the course.'

'Yes, sir.'

The deck plates vibrated a little faster under their feet as the liner accelerated towards the planet. On the screen the Drofen fleet was obvious in pursuit. Occasional shots from them struck the liner but its shields were just about holding. That was a relief because they were going to need those shields. Travelling faster than was sensible, the liner reached the upper edges of the planet's atmosphere. The ship shook violently and the view from the viewscreen became white hot.

'Shields holding,' a crewmember said.

'Even extended around the *Saint-Saens*?'

'Yes, sir.'

Watson gripped a console more tightly. He hadn't been sure they would get this far.

Three more blasts shook the liner.

'Drofen ships closing, sir.'

Two more hits.

'Let them close. How is our fleet?'

'Withdrawing from the planet.'

Well, that was something at least. 'Good. Time to release?'

'Eleven seconds, sir.'

Eleven seconds. Enough time to look at his crew, to see familiar faces as well as new ones he would get to know on future missions – if he got another ship. 'Time?'

'Three, two, one... released.'

A metallic clunk echoed through the ship signifying that the Saint-Saens had disengaged from the *Andromedan Princess*.

'All right,' Watson said, 'get us out of here.'

The *Saint-Saens* lurched violently as it was released and its overheating, dying engines tried to compensate, adjusting the ship's speed and trajectory. Its shields were also struggling against the last stages of re-entry.

A light flashed and an alarm pinged. Andy slapped a hand down to kill the safety cut outs.

Erimem had grabbed hold of the control panel with one hand and Adam's shirt with the other, dragging him to a place where he could hold the control panel too. The ship was vibrating uncontrollably.

Another safety cut-out flashed. This time it was Erimem who dismissed it.

Andy's eyes ran across the controls. It was an odd things. When she had learned to drive she had freaked out at moving between her dad's car and the instructor's. Things were just in different places on the dash or the wheel. She got used to dealing with the changes. Knowing about computers had made using more advanced computers – even those on a spaceship – easier. They tended to be intuitive and she could just about move from one to another. 'Andy Hansen, space pilot.'

'Did you mean to say that out loud?' Erimem asked.

'Oh... fudge,' Andy moaned. 'Sorry.' She extinguished the last failsafe and gripped the panel for dear life. 'We're through the upper atmosphere – just as well because the shields just died.'

'I could tell,' Erimem said. 'The ground is getting very close. I think we should go. Give me your hand. I don't have a travel ring.'

Andy extended a hand.

So did Adam.

Erimem took both of the outstretched hands and on her instruction, Andy and Adam twisted the central bands of their travel rings simultaneously. A spitting ball of electricity engulfed them and faded, taking them with it.

Vallaren emerged from his Citadel and looked up into the cloudless sky. A smoking black trail marred the sky. At its head was a great ball of flames, hurtling inexorably towards the surface, towards him. It was fire from the heavens. Vallaren relaxed and accepted the joy of the moment.

The fires would set him free.

A moment later, Vallaren ceased to exist.

The engines of the *Andromedan Princess* whined violently as the great liner strained to put as much distance between itself and the planet as possible. The screen showed the planet shrinking behind them but still too large and close for Watson's liking.

'One hundred and five percent of safe maximum,' Haniya reported. Her voice was admirably calm.

'Go to an hundred and ten,' Watson said evenly.

Haniya complied without any question.

The ship vibrated hard.

The screen flared white.

'Hold on,' Watson yelled.

The shockwave from the explosion reached the Drofen ships first. Many were close to the planet, others still accelerating towards their home. They all disintegrated as the wave of energy smashed into them. The wave caught up with the *Andromedan Princess* just over ten seconds later. The liner was moving quickly enough for Haniya to let the cruise ship be swept along by it rather than destroyed. By the time the wave reached the retreating Earth fleet, it gave them a violent shake but caused nothing more than minor damage.

On board his ship, Captain Watson realised that he had been holding his breath. He slowly exhaled and ordered the liner to fall into the fleet.

They had won. Well, a victory of sorts. Thousands had been lost from the liner and billions from the other Drofen attacks but they had brought that to an end.

It had cost his ship and more importantly it had cost the lives of three civilians, who had picked up weapons to fight under him. He had been captain of the *Saint-Saens*. He should have taken the ship on its last mission to the surface. He would struggle to forgive himself for letting those three young people die as they had.

'Is the ship still in one piece?'

Watson turned sharply. Erimem, Andy and Adam were standing in the doorway. 'You're alive!'

'I think so,' Erimem answered. 'Andy? Are you alive?'

'I'm definitely alive,' Andy answered, 'and I am in the mood to drink every bar on this tub dry.'

'This is a good plan,' Erimem nodded. 'We should get very, very drunk.'

'Amen to that,' Adam added.

They turned to leave but Watson called after them, 'How did you get off the *Saint-Saens*?'

Erimem smiled broadly. 'Magic.'

From the flight deck, Erimem led her party not to a bar but to the sickbay. Olivia wrapped Andy in a huge hug and kissed her until even Andy had to ask her to stop.

'Let me breathe, pirate!'

Erimem was met with hugs from Ibrahim and Helena, though Helena's was brief. She was still working on Captain Lescal's back. Lee appeared to be sedated, with her arm encased in a large metal tube. Tom greeted Adam with a firm handshake.

They all stayed together until Helena had done all she could and had put both of her patients under for a few hours.

When they were finally done, they fell on the executive bar on their deck and, with the exception of Helena and Ibrahim, who had taken temporary custody of baby Alex, they proceeded to have a damned good attempt at trying every drink in the bar. While everyone knew that Helena and Ibrahim wanted to start a family, Andy and Olivia were both surprised to find that they did, too. But that was a discussion for another day.

Erimem's party stayed on the *Andromedan Princess* for four days until it was able to dock at a military medical facility, helping with repairs and reports, and just being as useful as possible.

Arriving at the medical base was their cue to leave. There would be too many awkward questions to answer.

They watched Captain Lescal being taken away by a hover-porter floating stretcher. At her side, where she had been for the past four days, was Commander Lee, who carried little Alex in her newly repaired arm. Unless her gaydar was seriously off the mark, Andy was sure things had definitely thawed between Lee and Lescal.

Captain Watson was also disembarking, going to explain his actions. He would either be promoted or subject to a courts martial for deliberately destroying his own ship. He didn't seem bothered which way it went.

They gathered with their luggage in the bar to return home.

'Sorry this wasn't the trip we promised you, Tom,' Helena said.

Tom surprised them all with a smile. 'Are you kidding? This is the best time I've had in years. Thanks. I mean it. I did something useful and I actually felt like I was with friends. Thanks to you all for bringing me.'

'We promise no insane gods next time,' Helena said. 'Well, except Erimem of course.'

'I am sulking,' Erimem said, struggling to keep a smirk from her face.

They twisted their travel rings and once the electric storm had passed the bar was empty.

'Well done.'

Erimem was again sitting beside her grandfather, and again he was wearing his shades.

'It is dangerous to intercept me in travel like this,' she scolded.

Her grandfather snorted as if offended by her concern. 'Not for us,' he said. 'You did well, child. You closed a dangerous loop in time.'

Erimem humphed. 'We had to deal with a problem which only existed because we had to deal with that problem.'

'A closed loop,' her grandfather agreed. 'A very dangerous thing if it's not dealt with. You all did very well.'

'I know,' Erimem agreed, 'but I don't think Andy likes you very much. She did not like you going inside her mind.'

'I'm not surprised. It's a mess in there.' He smiled that kindly old smile she loved. 'I'm proud of you. You did well.'

Erimem blinked.

And she was arriving back in her Habitat with the others.

She relaxed.

* * *

Andy yawned massively and wandered into Erimem's enormous kitchen area. The doors were open out onto the terrace where an unbearably cute baby mammoth looked in. It wouldn't enter the house. They were artificially created constructs, more than projections but not quite "real" either, and so it was programmed to stay out of the villa.

Erimem was at the counter pouring orange juice. She looked tired and had a bad case of bed-head. 'Good morning,' she said sleepily.

'Yeah, 'morning,' Andy answered. 'You sleep okay?'

Erimem didn't look too sure about that. 'Sort of. A bit.'

'Ah,' said Andy, hoping she sounded wise. 'Thinking about a handsome Scottish copper, eh?'

'Something like that.'

'So, when will you be seeing...' she heard scuffing footsteps behind her and turned. Adam was sheepishly entering the kitchen wearing just a pair of pyjama trousers. '...Adam,' Andy finished lamely.

'Hi,' Adam said blearily. He took the orange juice Erimem passed to him. As he passed behind her there was just the slightest touch of his hand on her back and the smile that brought to Erimem's face was unmistakable.

'I think I'll take some OJ to Olivia,' Andy said. Erimem poured two glasses while Adam wandered across to greet the baby mammoth. Andy's voice dropped to a whisper. 'And you and I talk later,' she said, nodding pointedly at Adam.

'I don't know what you mean,' Erimem answered innocently.

Andy didn't utter a word. Her look was answer enough.

'Later,' Erimem conceded. 'Adam has to go to work soon.'

Andy sniffed. 'Guessing he's been at work all night,' she murmured.

Erimem's eyes went wide, her mouth opened in shock and then snapped shut again. She pushed two glasses of orange juice towards Andy. 'One more word and you wear these.'

Andy laughed heartily and headed for the door. 'See you later, kids. Be good.'

Heading up the stone steps to the room where Olivia was

sleeping, Andy felt a broad smile spread across her face. Her friend, her best friend, was happy. Adam was a good guy. He didn't deserve her, obviously, but he was still a good man. Smiling broadly, she hurried into the bedroom to share the news with Olivia.

EPILOGUE

Tom Niven dragged himself out of bed. Somebody had been knocking at his door for a few minutes. He had hoped they would just take the hint and go away but apparently that wasn't going to happen. He dragged himself to the door and opened it. 'Yeah?'

His mother pushed past him into the flat. 'What took you so long to answer?'

'I was in bed. Can't answer the door if I'm asleep.'

Tom didn't see his mother's hand move and only realised she had slapped him when pain exploded in his cheek. 'Do not be smart with me, Tom.'

'I'm sorry,' he said, a reflex from all the previous times he'd had to apologise without knowing why.

'So what happened?'

'We went to the future,' Tom answered. 'Hundreds of years. The aliens we saw in Stalingrad were...'

His mother cut him off. 'Do you know where the door to her Habitat is?'

Tom shook her head. 'She didn't tell me. She wouldn't let me keep a travel ring either.'

'She doesn't trust you,' his mother said sourly. He had failed again.

'Not yet, but I'm travelling with them again.' He sounded desperate. She always made him feel like that. 'I made friends with Andy... Andrea. Helena and Ibrahim like me. So does Adam. I think he's Erimem's boyfriend.'

'Boyfriend?' That interested his mother. 'That's new, useful.' She thought. 'They're suspicious, but you made progress.' There was no hint of praise in her words. 'Stay with them, ingratiate yourself.' He saw the second slap coming but knew better than to flinch. 'But don't take long. I sent you to this wretched school in this miserable country for a reason. We want that freedom to travel in time. We've planned this for a long time. It's the only reason you're here.' She headed back to the door. 'Clean this place up. It's a mess.' The door closed behind her.

Tom looked at the closed door. Well, that was a metaphor for every bit of his relationship with his mother. When she said that ingratiating himself with Erimem was the only reason he was there, she wasn't talking about being at the university. If she hadn't needed someone to go to the uni at this time – and it being a blood relative made her more powerful in her organisation – Tom know that he would never have been born.

That might have been the better option.

If she had cared enough to hate him that would have been better. She didn't even give him that much.

Tom sank back on his bed.

Yeah, he thought, it would have been better if he had never been born.